Emmy's nerves beg
"Mac? What's happ

"Then you feel it, too." His thumb stroked across her cheek. "This heat between us."

Unable to speak, captivated by the caress of his thumb and the pull of those dark eyes, she nodded.

"What I'm feeling—it's dangerous."

And impossible to fight. Wanting, needing his lips against hers, Emmy rose on her toes and looped her arms around his neck.

"Emmy—" he warned, and started to untangle her arms.

"Don't. Just kiss me."

Dear Reader,

This is the fourth and final book of the Halo Island miniseries. This story features Emmy Logan, a new arrival in town, and Mac Struthers, the man remodeling the kitchen of the house across the street.

Divorced Emmy has her hands full with a rebellious eleven-year-old son. Mac, who raised his twin brothers and will soon leave town, wants nothing to do with the attractive single mother or her son. But then… Well, you'll find out when you read the book. ☺

Keep those e-mails and letters coming—I love hearing from you. E-mail me at ann@annroth.net, or write to me at Ann Roth, P.O. Box 25003, Seattle, WA 98165-1903. Also, please visit my Web site at www.annroth.net and enter the monthly contest to win a free book. You'll also find my latest writing news and a new, delicious recipe posted every month.

Happy reading!

Ann Roth

A Father for Jesse

ANN ROTH

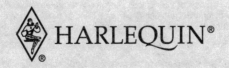

HARLEQUIN®

TORONTO • NEW YORK • LONDON
AMSTERDAM • PARIS • SYDNEY • HAMBURG
STOCKHOLM • ATHENS • TOKYO • MILAN • MADRID
PRAGUE • WARSAW • BUDAPEST • AUCKLAND

To Carol Morris, a courageous and tenacious woman.
You are loved!

Recycling programs
for this product may
not exist in your area.

ISBN-13: 978-0-373-75270-6

A FATHER FOR JESSE

Copyright © 2009 by Ann Schuessler.

www.eHarlequin.com

Printed in U.S.A.

ABOUT THE AUTHOR

Ann Roth lives in the greater Seattle area with her husband. After earning an MBA she worked as a banker and corporate trainer. She gave up the corporate life to write, and if they awarded PhDs in writing happily-ever-after stories, she'd surely have one.

Ann loves to hear from readers. You can write her at P.O. Box 25003, Seattle, WA 98165-1903 or e-mail her at ann@annroth.net.

Books by Ann Roth

HARLEQUIN AMERICAN ROMANCE
1031—THE LAST TIME WE KISSED
1103—THE BABY INHERITANCE
1120—THE MAN SHE'LL MARRY
1159—IT HAPPENED ONE WEDDING
1174—MITCH TAKES A WIFE
1188—ALL I WANT FOR CHRISTMAS
1204—THE PILOT'S WOMAN
1252—OOH, BABY!

Don't miss any of our special offers. Write to us at the following address for information on our newest releases.

Harlequin Reader Service
U.S.: 3010 Walden Ave., P.O. Box 1325, Buffalo, NY 14269
Canadian: P.O. Box 609, Fort Erie, Ont. L2A 5X3

EMMY'S BROWNIES

Preheat the oven to 350°F. Grease a 9" x 12" pan.
In a double boiler melt:

> 3 oz semisweet chocolate
> 2 oz unsweetened chocolate
> 3 sticks butter

Set aside to cool slightly.
Combine and set aside the following:

> 2/3 cup flour, sifted
> 1 tsp baking powder

In a mixing bowl beat:

> 6 eggs
> 2 cups sugar

Add chocolate mixture. Slowly mix in the dry
ingredients. Add 1 tsp vanilla and 2 cups chopped
pecans and mix well.

Pour into prepared pan. Bake 30-40 minutes. Cool, cut
into squares. May be refrigerated.

Chapter One

The windshield wipers barely kept up with the steady downpour. Emmy Logan slowed to a crawl and gripped the wheel of her aging sedan, which was harder to steer with the U-Haul trailer behind it. Two-lane Treeline Road was all but deserted, and if not for the houses peeking through the woods on either side, a person could easily think she was alone here. Dark and gloomy as it was, today, January third, was the start of a new year and a new life.

"Isn't Halo Island beautiful?" she asked, casting an anxious glance at her eleven-year-old son.

Jesse shrugged his narrow shoulders. "It's raining and it's cold and there aren't any stores."

"We're in the Pacific Northwest. It's *supposed* to rain in January. Remember, this is a small town of less than two thousand people—nothing like Oakland. Most of the shops are downtown, which isn't far from here. Once we're settled in, I'll take you."

The rural setting was one reason Emmy had chosen Halo Island. She'd first visited in November to interview for a librarian position and had instantly fallen in love with the place and its friendly people.

More important, the town was worlds away from Tyrell Barker, leader of the Street Kings, the neighborhood gang that had courted her young, fatherless son. Since Tyrell and his teenage thug buddies had befriended Jesse, her son had grown hostile and difficult to control. His grades suffered, and he was frequently called to the principal's office. Emmy tried cajoling, threats and even bribery to get him to behave, but nothing worked.

The final, frightening straw was the gun Tyrell had loaned Jesse. Emmy had had no idea until after Jesse gave it back, and she'd only found out because she'd eavesdropped on one of her son's phone conversations. After that, the only choice was to move. Here on Halo Island, she hoped her son would quickly forget the gang, make friends with decent kids and get back on track.

Jesse yawned, and small wonder. Driving almost nine hundred miles from Oakland to Anacortes, then waiting for and catching the ferry to Halo Island—a forty-five-minute trip—made for a long two days. They hadn't even celebrated the new year.

"Are we there yet?" he asked.

"According to MapQuest, Beach Cove Way—our street—should be somewhere along here on the left side of the road. So keep an eye out."

Jesse squinted through the windshield, then nodded at a green road sign several hundred yards ahead. "Maybe that's it."

"Must be." Emmy tapped the brakes. A moment later she could read the sign, which had a painted white gull hanging beneath it. Beach Cove Way. "You're so good at finding things. I don't know what I'd do without your help."

"Whatever," Jesse mumbled, but he brightened up.

Signaling, Emmy turned down the narrow, winding road. Among the fir trees were several charming cottages. According to their landlords, the Rutherfords, most of the houses on the street were vacant until the summer tourist season. The Rutherfords and now Emmy and Jesse were the only people living here.

As they rounded a bend seconds later they glimpsed the ocean between the trees. Finally, near the end of the cul-de-sac, they found their cottage.

"There it is, our new home." Emmy pulled into the short, gravel driveway and cut the engine. With the rain falling fast and furious, they were sure to get drenched. "Let's sit here a minute and see if the storm lets up," she said.

As the downpour thundered on the car roof, her son silently took in the neat, white cottage, the small yard, and the beach and ocean beyond.

"What do you think?" she prodded.

"It's okay, I guess, but I'd rather be in Oakland with my buds."

Gang members hardly counted as friends, but Emmy refrained from saying so. She'd only upset Jesse, and she was determined to do everything possible to make his transition pleasant. "I miss my friends, too," she said. "But I'm going to make new ones. So will you."

"Not if I don't want to." Jess crossed his arms and compressed his lips. "The only people I need are back in Oakland. I want to go home."

"That life is behind us," she said firmly. "Halo Island is our home. We're practically on the beach. I think that's pretty special."

"For a vacation, maybe. I don't want to *live* here."

"But I have a wonderful job with the Halo Island Library. Things aren't as expensive here as they are in Oakland, so we won't have to worry so much about money. That means when you need something, I'll probably be able to get it for you." She'd still be careful, though. The move had drained most of her savings.

"That's good," Jesse said, but Emmy could tell something was bothering him.

"What is it?" she asked.

"What if my dad wants to find me?"

The yearning look on his face about broke her heart. "I don't think that's going to happen, Jesse. He's been gone six whole years now, and we haven't heard from him once."

"But what if he changes his mind?"

"He knows how to get hold of Grandma or Grandpa. They both have our address. But don't get your hopes up."

"I hate him, anyway."

Emmy didn't like Chas much, either. She wondered what she'd ever seen in her former husband. He'd married her because she was pregnant—a big mistake since, from the start, he'd cheated on her. Determined to make the home she'd always dreamed of with a loving husband at her side, she'd doggedly stuck with Chas. Couple's counseling had helped for a few years. But Chas was a restless soul who believed he was meant to roam the world without cares or concerns. Certainly he'd never wanted marriage or children. In a single afternoon he filed for divorce, cleaned out their bank account and disappeared. Leaving her basically penniless, with a five-year-old son to support. An attorney had handled all correspondence, and Emmy hadn't heard from Chas since. The child support he owed was staggering, and his refusal to contact Jess even more devastating. But she'd already wasted too much time cursing her ex-husband.

For a brief period after the divorce, battered but still clinging to her dreams of a loving spouse, she'd dated a few guys, never bringing anyone home. That way if nothing came of the date, Jesse wouldn't get attached. Nothing ever did, and after a year of dead-end dinners and movies, she'd stopped trying. She no longer believed in happily ever after. Now her focus centered on her son and his well-being. Jesse and work filled her life, and that was enough.

As the storm relentlessly pounded the car, she buttoned her coat. "Doesn't sound as if the rain will stop anytime soon, and I'm dying to see our house." She pulled up her hood and opened her door. "Zip your jacket, and let's make a run for the Rutherfords' and pick up our key." Emmy had never met the couple, only spoken with them on the phone, but she knew they lived just across the street.

As she and Jesse sprinted through the wet, brown grass, he actually giggled. A bubbling sound that had Emmy smiling despite the weather.

The Rutherfords' house was about twice the size of the cottage, and beautiful. Standing on their large, covered porch, Emmy wiped her feet on the mat. Jesse did the same.

She brushed at her wet face, pulled off her hood and took a deep breath. "Just smell the ocean!"

Jess sniffed. She rang the doorbell. Moments later the door opened. A plump, sixtysomething woman in a sweater and flowered skirt greeted them with a warm smile.

"You must be Emmy and Jesse. I'm Melinda Rutherford. Welcome to Halo Island and the hardest rain I've seen in months. Please come in. You'll have to excuse the mess—we're about to have our kitchen remodeled."

As they stepped into a large, cluttered living room, a graying Burl Ives of a man in a flannel shirt, suspenders and an expression that matched his wife's, saluted. "I'm Tom Rutherford. Glad you finally made it. Looks as if you got a little wet. Don't worry, by late April the rain will stop till October or so. Until then, prepare to grow webbed feet." He winked at Jesse. "How old are you, son?"

"Eleven."

"That's what? Fifth grade?"

Jesse nodded. Monday he started at Halo Island School, which went from kindergarten through high school.

"You'll be in Mrs. Hatcher's class. She's real nice. A good teacher—and pretty, too. You'll like her."

"She impressed me when we spoke on the phone," Emmy said. She'd know more when she met the woman in person Tuesday afternoon. She tipped her chin Jesse's way. "It's great to hear all those positive things about your teacher, huh?"

Her son nodded, his eyes wide as he took in the kitchen table and stacked chairs. Dishes, cookbooks, small appliances and other cookware were piled on every available surface.

"I'm afraid it'll be like this for the next six weeks," Melinda said. "That's how long this renovation should take."

"Unless there are problems." Tom hooked his thumbs around his suspenders. "I'm guessing more like two or three months."

"Mac's leaving town. He already bought his plane ticket, remember? He'll be done on time."

"Mac's our contractor," Tom explained. "Once he finishes with us he'll travel Europe for a few months. Come summer, he's off to college in Seattle."

Their contactor sounded young to be tackling such a huge project, Emmy thought.

"We're enlarging the room by several feet, which will cut into the backyard," Melinda said. "Since our kids are grown and living off the island, we don't need all that grass, anyway. I love to cook—we're getting top-of-the-line appliances and a roomy breakfast nook." She rubbed her hands together. "When the place is finished, we'll have you over for dinner."

"That'd be lovely." The friendly couple were the answer to Emmy's prayers. She envisioned growing close, the Rutherfords becoming surrogate grandparents to Jesse. Emmy's parents, long divorced, rarely visited, and Chas's were both dead. "In the meantime, once I'm settled, *I'll* have *you* over."

Tom nodded. "We'd appreciate that." At the sound of an engine, audible despite the closed windows, he glanced at his watch. "There's Mac now. He starts work Monday and wants to review the final plans."

"Then we'll be on our way," Emmy said. "If you'll just give us the key…"

"Got that right here." Tom extracted the key from his pocket and handed it to her. "I'll be over later to help you move your things into the house."

Since the cottage came mostly furnished, there wasn't that much to unload—suitcases, boxes, framed pictures, Jesse's posters and a few small pieces of furniture. Used to doing things for herself, Emmy shook her head. "We don't have anything especially heavy. We'll manage."

"Independent sort, aren't you? If you change your mind, let me know."

"You may as well stay and meet Mac," Melinda said. "Since he'll be in and out every day for the next six weeks, you're sure to run into each other."

Seconds later a firm rap sounded on the door.

The man who stepped through it was no teenage boy. He looked about Emmy's age—thirty. He was tall and solid with a broad forehead, straight nose and strong jaw, and dark, curly hair in need of a trim. He wore loose, faded jeans, a black T-shirt and a denim jacket that hugged his broad shoulders.

In a word, gorgeous.

"Mac Struthers, meet our new tenant, Emmy Logan, and her son, Jesse."

Jesse nodded, and though he said nothing, Emmy could tell he was impressed. Small wonder. It wasn't every day a person met a man with such presence.

Holding a black leather portfolio, the contractor turned to Emmy, his gaze flicking over her. "Pleasure."

She managed a cool smile, at odds with her fluttery nerves. "Hello."

He towered over her. His grip was firm and warm. And his vividly blue eyes… Cheeks heating, Emmy glanced away.

Next, Mac extended his hand to her son. "Nice to meet you, Jesse."

Looking as if he very much wanted to be a man, Jesse solemnly shook hands. "You, too, Mr. Struthers."

"Mr. Struthers was my father." Mac's mouth quirked. "Everyone calls me Mac."

Utterly charmed, and confused at this man's effect on her, Emmy placed her hand on Jesse's shoulder. "Time for us to start moving in. It was nice meeting you all. Goodbye."

BY THE TIME Mac left the Rutherfords' place an hour later, the rain had stopped. Pausing on the porch with only the sound of water dripping from the trees filling the crisp, silent air, he jotted down a few final notes on things to do between now and Monday morning. Pick up supplies and load the van with—

A woman's laugh, as pretty and light as butterfly wings, interrupted his thoughts. Followed by a boy's chuckle. The sounds were contagious and Mac smiled. The porch faced the water, and fir trees blocked any direct view of the woman and boy, but if he angled his head and peered through the branches he could see them without being spotted.

He watched Emmy heft a box from the U-Haul, hand it to Jesse, then grab another for herself.

She was a looker, and Mac looked his fill. Her light brown, straight hair hung an inch or so shy of her shoulders and suited her pretty features. Her short winter jacket and snug jeans showed off long, slender legs and a round backside. Mac imagined her in tight, skimpy shorts. Better yet, a lacy thong… His body stirred. Then he caught himself and frowned.

A single mom with a young son? Count him out. He'd already raised kids—his twin brothers. They'd been ten, almost the same age as Jesse was now, when their parents had died in a car crash. Mac had been all of eighteen, about to graduate from high school, with big plans to travel through Europe, then head for college and a degree in architecture. But after the accident, everything changed.

While his friends lazed away their post-high-school-graduation summer, then started college, pledged fraternities and dated cute coeds, Mac had looked after his brothers, worked on a construction crew and kept house. Not easy, but he'd seen Ian and Brian through eight years of school. By the time they finished high school, he'd started his own home-remodeling business. Money earned from that, plus proceeds from the sale of their parents' house, had covered the twins' college education. Summers they worked for him, earning a paycheck and learning the business. This past December they'd both graduated. Mac was proud as hell of them.

And ready to realize his own ambitions. Finally, at the ripe old age of thirty, it was his turn. As soon as he finished redoing the Rutherford kitchen, he planned to travel around Europe for a few months. With no set agenda and no responsibilities, he could go wherever he wanted, as carefree as he'd always dreamed of being. He'd fly back in time for summer quarter at the University of Washington. Mac wanted the degree, which his parents had urged him to earn, and the kind of interaction you could only get in a classroom. He meant to get a bachelor degree in construction management. By doubling up on credits and taking classes year-round, he figured he'd finish in just under three years. While he was gone, his brothers would run the company and finance his education, just as he'd done for them.

This time, nothing short of death would stop him. Nothing.

"I'm tired," he heard Jesse say.

"I know," his mother replied. "Let's hurry and bring in

the rest of the boxes before the rain starts again. Then we'll return the U-Haul—if we get it back before five, we save money—pick up something for dinner and relax."

"I gonna relax *now*."

"There isn't that much left to do. If we work together, we'll finish in no time. *Then* you can goof off."

The boy crossed his arms and shook his head.

"Please? Just a little more?"

"Uh-uh. I'm quitting *now*."

"Come on, Jess, I really need your help."

"No. *N. O.*"

Mac eyed the defiant boy, who clearly needed a firm hand. Which, judging by his mother's pleading voice and expression, was something she didn't understand.

"What'll it take to change your mind?" she asked in a soft voice. "Ice cream? A new T-shirt?"

Jesse snorted and shook his head. "You can't make me do what I don't want to do. You can't make me do *anything*." His chin jutted out in challenge. "I hate it here. I want to move back home to Oakland, and my friends."

A loud breath huffed from Emmy's lips, as if she was trying to hold on to her temper. "We've already discussed this numerous times. We're not going back. *This* is our home now."

"Not mine. I never wanted to move, and I'll never like it here. I. Want. To. Go. Back," Jesse repeated, emphasizing every word.

"If you just give Halo Island a chance, I know—"

"You *don't* know. This place is lame and so are you. I hate you!" He spit out the words. "You can just…go to hell."

Looking shocked and hurt, Emmy recoiled. "What did you say?"

"I said, I hate you and go to hell."

The kid had just stepped over the line. Without stopping to think, Mac headed toward him and his mother.

I HATE YOU and go to hell. Jesse's stinging zinger sliced straight into Emmy's heart. Crushed, appalled at his nerve and a little scared, she made her you'd-better-take-that-back-or-you're-in-trouble face. Seemingly unfazed, he stared sullenly at her. She realized she'd completely lost the ability to control him. *Dear God, what to do now?*

Out of the corner of her eye she caught a whir of movement. Mac strode across the yard, his jaw tight and his gaze narrowed on Jesse. As he closed the distance between them, her son dropped the tough pose. Suddenly a little boy again, he shuffled his feet.

Mac stopped not a foot away, his big hands low on his hips. "No boy should talk to his mother like that," he said in a quiet but commanding voice. In the cold, his breath formed sharp clouds. "You apologize to her."

To Emmy's amazement, her rebellious son gave a meek nod.

"Sorry," he grumbled, chewing his cheek.

She nodded.

"That's more like it." Mac's expression lightened. "Now do like your mother asked and help with those boxes."

Lips tight, Jesse hurried to comply.

While Emmy was relieved to have his cooperation again, she was embarrassed that Mac had heard Jess's awful words. She was also furious at this man she didn't even know, telling her child how to behave.

She waited until Jesse disappeared into the house, then rounded on Mac. "Just who do you think you are?"

Clearly surprised, he put his hands up, palms out. "Hey, I was only trying to help. I know kids, and if you don't make them toe the line now, you'll lose them later."

How did Mac figure that? He was probably right. Heaven knew she wasn't the best at making Jesse behave. That needed to change. But this virtual stranger disciplining *her* son—it was too much.

"You don't even know us, and you certainly have no right to butt into our lives," she said, seething. "So butt out."

Mac flinched as if she'd slapped him. Verbally, she had.

"It won't happen again." Turning on his heel, he walked away.

Chapter Two

For the rest of the weekend, while Emmy and Jesse grocery shopped, bought paint for Jesse's bedroom and unpacked boxes, she thought about Mac and what he'd said. Also what *she'd* said. In hindsight she realized he'd only meant to help. Which he *had*—Jess had pretty much behaved since. And how had she thanked Mac? By bawling him out. She couldn't stop thinking about the startled look on his face and how he drew back. Her uncivil behavior gnawed at her so that even when she fell into bed exhausted late at night, she couldn't sleep.

By Monday morning, sick of beating up on herself, she made a decision. When Mac showed up at the Rutherfords' today, she'd march over there and apologize. The very thought salved her conscience.

At the moment, though, there were bigger concerns—for one, convincing Jesse to go to school. After that one frightening moment Saturday afternoon, she no longer feared she'd lost control. She and Jess were back on track with their usual tug-of-war, but she did have the final say and he knew it. Thank goodness. Even if the constant arguing drained her.

"Do I have to go?" he asked, head bowed over his still-empty cereal bowl.

Like her he was tired, but that wasn't the real reason for his balky behavior. Shy by nature, he didn't adapt easily to change.

Now in the small kitchen, sitting across the square wood table from him, Emmy sipped her coffee and tried to ease his fears. "Remember what Mr. Rutherford said? Mrs. Hatcher's really nice."

"Then she won't mind if I'm not there today."

"But she's expecting you."

"Come on, Mom, second semester hasn't even started yet. They'll probably be reviewing for their finals. I already finished my first semester, so me going today is lame."

Not really. Jesse needed the time to adjust to his teacher and classroom, and hopefully start making friends. Emmy arched her eyebrows. "You're going to school, period." Hating that she sounded so stern, she added, "But if you want, I'll drive you."

"No way!" He looked mortified. "I'll catch the bus."

Which meant that he wasn't going to fight her any more about school. She'd won the first battle of the day, a big relief. She glanced at the brass ship's clock, a thirtieth birthday gift from her father that now decorated the kitchen wall. "Which will be here in less than half an hour. You'd better eat breakfast while you have time."

Jesse poured cornflakes into his bowl, then added sugar and milk. That he didn't want a ride—didn't want to be seen with his *mother*—was nothing new. He was growing up—way too fast for Emmy. She remembered herself at his age, wanting to be independent yet still needing her mother. A woman who was remote and distracted and only too eager to push Emmy out of the nest. Her father had been far more affectionate, but after her parents divorced when Emmy was six, he'd moved to the East Coast. Growing up, she only saw him a few times a year. Now, with money tight, she saw him even less.

Jesse attacked his cereal as if he hadn't eaten in days. Lately he was always hungry, yet never seemed to gain weight.

Deep in thought, Emmy poured herself a smaller portion. She worked hard to be the opposite of her mother, to be here whenever her son needed her and also when he didn't—just in case. To listen and help and be the mom she'd always wanted. She would explain this to Mac so that he understood, she decided as she ate. The man no doubt thought she was a shrew. Emmy cringed at that.

Then again, why did she even care? She certainly wasn't interested in him. *No? Then why am I spending so much time worrying about his opinion of me?*

Because she wanted him, and everyone else in town, to like her. She wanted to fit in and set down roots here.

Checking the clock a second time, she sprang into action. "The bus will be here really soon. Better wash your face and brush your teeth."

While Jesse did so in their microscopic bathroom, Emmy cleared the table, loaded the dishwasher and sponged up her son's dribbled milk and cereal. She probably should ask him to clean up his own mess, but didn't want him to miss the bus.

If you don't make them toe the line now, you'll lose them later, Mac had said. Did that apply to dishes, too? She'd make Jesse do the dinner dishes.

How did Mac know that, anyway? Had he been a

handful for his parents? Or maybe he had a child or two of his own. Was he married? Divorced? Emmy wanted to know, but wouldn't ask—didn't want him to think she was too interested.

Jesse returned to the kitchen with his face washed and his hair gelled and styled like many boys his age. In contrast to his movie-star-cool hair, he wore the clothes Tyrell and his posse favored—a black oversize T-shirt with the Street King's emblem of a hand-drawn red crown on the front and a red skull and crossbones on the back. His black jeans were so loose they could fall down at any moment and his sneakers were unlaced. Emmy hated that her son still owned the awful T-shirt. She detested the entire outfit, which was sure to make a poor first impression at school. They might even send a note home, asking that he not wear these clothes. Half hoping they would, biting the inside of her cheek to keep from sending Jesse back to his room to change—she didn't want to fight this battle now, especially when he was running late—she handed him his lunch money.

Jesse pocketed the three dollars and turned away. "Bye, Mom."

"Don't I rate a kiss?"

He was still a few inches shorter than she was, and Emmy bent her head. Rolling his eyes, Jesse gave her a quick peck. She fought the urge to pull him into a hug. He wouldn't like that.

Bypassing the walnut coat tree they'd brought from Oakland, he headed toward the door. Why did kids think it cool to go coatless and shiver all day?

"Wait just a minute," Emmy said. "It's January. You need your jacket."

With an audible sigh of irritation, he grabbed his

bomber jacket. He shrugged into it, then swung his backpack over one shoulder.

Much better. Emmy smiled. "If you change your mind and want me to pick you up after school, call. I'll be here, painting your room." Her new job started a week from today, giving her seven whole days to spruce up the house and make it into a home. And five days to be here for Jesse after school, instead of making him come to the library and wait for her shift to end.

"I'll ride the bus back," he said.

"Would you like me to wait with you this morning?"

He looked appalled at the very idea. "Mo-om."

"I was only offering. Bye."

He clomped through the door, banging it shut it behind him. Suddenly the cottage was much too quiet. Chafing her arms against a surge of loneliness, Emmy stood in the living room and peeked through a chink in the drapes, spying shamelessly as her son waited at the end of the driveway. The morning was damp, chill and gray, and she was glad she'd made him wear his jacket.

Moments later the bus rounded the bend and rolled toward the house. As it screeched and stopped, Emmy noted several boys and girls seated inside. Would one or more of them become Jesse's friends?

She hoped so. "Be happy today, heart of my heart," she murmured.

The bus driver, a man with a round face and friendly smile, greeted Jesse. Emmy couldn't see her son's expression, but his shoulders were straight, instead of slumped—a positive sign, right? Jess boarded and disappeared inside.

Not five seconds after the bus rumbled off, Mac's white van pulled to a stop on the far side of the Rutherfords' driveway. He certainly started work early.

Emmy's spirits lifted, which was ridiculous. At the same time, for some reason, she was suddenly nervous about apologizing. She continued to peek through the drapes, watching as Mac unfolded his long legs and exited the van. No jacket today, just a dark T-shirt. Good thing Jess wasn't here to see that.

He took the front steps two at a time, crossed the porch and knocked on the Rutherfords' door. Shortly after Mac disappeared inside, Emmy's landlords left the house and drove away. They owned Rutherford Boat Repair in town. Melinda had told Emmy about their shop and about leaving first thing in the morning when she'd stopped by yesterday with a welcome-to-the-cottage pound of coffee and the remodeling plans. Emmy could only dream of such a beautiful new kitchen, and wondered at the skill and effort required to create it.

Mac returned to the van, and she absently fluffed her hair. He pulled open the sliding doors, then lugged load after load of materials onto the porch, his breath huffing in clouds and his biceps bulging. No wonder he looked so strong and fit. Probably had abs of steel, too. And his legs… Even in loose jeans she noted his powerful thighs.

Hand at her throat, she blew out an admiring breath. What would Carla, her best friend in Oakland, say about Mac? No doubt she'd lick her lips and fan herself. What red-blooded woman wouldn't?

Emmy couldn't see inside the van, but surely by now it must be nearly empty. She'd talk to him before he went inside for good.

After putting on lipstick, then wiping it off—don't want to give him the wrong idea—Emmy checked her hair. She slipped on her coat, then corralling her nervousness, headed out the door.

HAULING SUPPLIES onto the Rutherfords' porch was hard work, and after a dozen trips Mac had worked up a light sweat. His hands were cold, though, and standing beside the stack of drywall, he blew on his fists with clouded breath. And wondered when his brothers would show up with the Dumpster. Once they arrived, they'd start gutting the kitchen, a huge job sure to take the entire day.

He started down the steps to get his circular saw and spotted Emmy Logan headed his way, her hair tucked behind her ears and her coat buttoned up tight. Like before, she wore jeans and ankle boots. No smile, but no frown, either. Which could mean anything. Remembering the other day and not about to get on her bad side again, Mac kept his expression carefully neutral and his mouth shut. She reached the van the same time he did.

Cautious, his arms at his sides, he eyed her.

"Um, good morning," she said, stuffing her gloved hands into her coat pockets.

"Morning." During the seconds that ticked by, time he could be transporting his tools, he cocked his eyebrows. "Did you want something?"

"I…" She glanced down. "I'm here to apologize for my behavior the other day."

He hadn't expected this. "Really."

She nodded. "You were trying to help. I shouldn't have snapped at you."

She'd done more than snap. With her eyes flashing and her fearless, defensive stance she'd reminded him of a mama bear defending her cub. Who was no cub, but a boy badly in need of discipline. In Mac's book a big part of good parenting. But Emmy was a single mom, probably doing the best she could.

"And I had no right wading in where I wasn't invited. Apology accepted."

"Thank you."

Her shoulders relaxed a bit. That and the relief on her face were another surprise. Was this apology so important to her?

"You seem to know something about kids," she said. "You and your wife must have one or two."

Either the sudden pink in her cheeks was from the cold or she was blushing. *Interesting.* "Never been married," Mac said. "And I don't have any kids. Don't plan to, either."

"Oh. Well."

He could see that she had more questions. "What do you want to know?" he asked.

"I'm wondering how it is that a single man without children knows so much about them. Not that it's any of my business." She shoved her hands deeper into her pockets, as if flustered.

For some reason Mac found that sweet—go figure. "It's no secret," he said. "Our parents died when I was eighteen and my twin brothers were ten. I raised them. That's why I don't want kids of my own. I've already played daddy."

"You took care of your two brothers all by yourself?" She looked at him, amazed. "I'm a thirty-year-old woman. Taking care of one child is hard for me. You were only eighteen, still a boy yourself. How in the world did you manage?"

"By growing up real fast. There was insurance money. We used most of it to pay off the house. That helped." But making ends meet, providing his brothers with food, clothing and school supplies, had been a struggle. Not to mention keeping them on the straight and narrow.

"It takes more than money to raise kids. It can't have been easy."

Her face radiated compassion. Nothing new there. Over the years Mac had heard his share of *I'm sorrys* and *how sads* from people who simply mouthed the words. Emmy's sympathy seemed genuinely heartfelt. Maybe because she was a single parent with challenges of her own.

"You have no idea," he said.

"So that's why you waited to start college until now."

"Actually, summer quarter starts in mid-June. I'm going to Europe first, then heading to Seattle."

"Quitting your job and traveling sounds wonderful," she said, flashing her even, white teeth.

Her first genuine smile. That and her suddenly sparkling eyes brightened the gray morning.

"Don't I know it." He grinned back. "But I'm not quitting—just taking a few years off. After I get my degree, I'll be back. While I'm gone, my kid brothers, Brian and Ian, will run the business."

They'd offered without Mac even asking. He knew why. They owed him. Which was true, but he wouldn't have agreed unless they really wanted to run the company. Both assured him they did. A good thing, since they were the best hands he'd ever hired.

"I never had brothers or sisters," Emmy said in a wistful tone. "You're lucky."

Even without the smile she was so pretty Mac couldn't look away. Her eyes were green. And warm. Maybe she liked him a little. He liked her, too. If he hadn't been leaving town soon and she hadn't had a kid, he'd seriously consider asking her for a date. Except she was probably looking for a husband. No, thanks. Mac was tired of being Mr. Responsible. Six weeks and counting until he was out of here and free. This morning was nothing but a friendly conversation with a woman who also happened to be beautiful.

He tore his gaze from her. "Sometimes brothers are a real pain," he said, rolling his eyes skyward.

"Even so, I'll bet you're never lonely. I always wanted Jesse to have a brother or sister, but it didn't work out."

Mac had to know. Not because he cared—he couldn't afford to go there—but because he was curious. "Where's his dad?"

"Gone." Emmy's eyes went flat. "Jesse was five when Chas filed for divorce, emptied the bank account and disappeared. He didn't even surface to sign the divorce papers—his attorney handled everything. You don't want to know how much he owes in child support."

A bum deal for sure. No wonder the boy was such a handful. Neither he nor his mom had had an easy time.

"Bastard."

"He is, but Jesse and I are managing."

She raised her chin defensively, and Mac knew that this was not a woman who accepted help easily. Which he totally understood, since he was the same way.

"Speaking of Jesse, I saw him catch the bus this morning." He wouldn't say what he thought of the kid's gangsta dress style. He didn't want Emmy shooting daggers at him again.

"Today is his first day at school. He takes a while to adjust to new things and he was nervous. I offered him a ride, but he insisted on taking the bus." The smile

Mac so liked twitched Emmy's lips. "That's my Jess, Mr. Independent. I hope he likes school and his teacher, Mrs. Hatcher. Tom Rutherford said good things about her."

A light breeze stirred up her hair, and little wisps fluttered around her face. Mac shoved his hands into the hip pockets of his jeans to keep from reaching out and brushing them back.

"I know Liza," he said. "Her husband, D.J., owns Island Air and last year he and Liza hired me to remodel their upstairs. She's great. Friendly and nurturing. From what I hear, kids love her."

"That's great news. My son needs a caring teacher and a positive school experience." Her eyes filled with shadows.

"Bad year?"

Hugging herself, Emmy nodded. "An older boy—a street-gang leader—befriended Jesse and tried to recruit him. That's why we left Oakland."

And explained the boy's clothes this morning.

"What you said about teaching kids things at a young age—you're absolutely right." Emmy's frank expression held Mac like a tether. "And I swear, I'm going to—"

A horn tooted, cutting off whatever she was about to say. Mac's brothers had arrived. Their shiny black truck pulled to a stop several yards away. The dingy red tow truck behind them rumbled on, slowly backing the Dumpster into the driveway.

Standing here talking with Emmy, Mac had completely forgotten about work. Which just showed how cockeyed he was this morning. Frowning, he watched the tow truck position and deposit the Dumpster, pull out of the driveway and trundle away.

And had a stern talk with himself. He was *not* interested in Emmy Logan. *Was not.* But she sure attracted him. Those big, expressive eyes, that generous mouth, those long, slender legs… His body tightened, and he bit back an oath. No more of that.

His brothers slid out of both sides of their vehicle and slammed the doors. They grabbed tools from the back.

"Looks as if your help has arrived," Emmy said. "Are those your brothers?" She sounded ready for more easy back-and-forth.

Not Mac. This conversation was over. So was his interest in her—or it would be once he got busy working. "Yep," he said, hardening his mouth.

His tone was harsh, and judging by the sudden jump of Emmy's eyebrows, unexpected.

Best this way. Mac didn't want her thinking they were friends when they weren't.

MAC'S HOSTILE expression and clipped reply told Emmy he wanted her gone. After their enjoyable conversation, the sudden dismissal both stung and confused her. She glanced at the two grinning males sauntering slowly their way. "Is it them or me who put that frown on your face?"

"I'm not frowning."

Oh, yes, he was. Apparently he didn't like her and had tired of pretending he did. Why not just say he needed to get to work?

"I know you're busy. I also have things to do, so I'll go." She wanted to paint Jesse's entire room before the bus dropped him off after school.

But she also wanted to meet the men Mac had raised. Who looked almost identical and bore a striking resemblance to their brother, though their faces were leaner and younger. Both openly scrutinized Emmy from head to toe. Self-conscious, she straightened her spine and sucked in her stomach, even though that part of her was hidden under her buttoned wool jacket.

"Before I go, could you introduce me to your brothers?" she asked.

Who, by their matching curious expressions, wanted to meet her, too.

"I don't have much choice," Mac muttered, looking as if he'd rather eat nails. "Otherwise they'll wonder who you are. That could lead to some serious razzing."

"You're joking." Though Mac's unhappy face told her he wasn't. "There's nothing about me to wonder over. Or about us. We're talking, that's all."

Emmy was proud of her nonchalant tone. Mac would never know she was attracted to him. She was strong-willed, and could and would banish her feelings. Getting settled, helping Jesse adjust and being busy with her new job would see to that. She didn't want to get involved with any man, least of all one who was leaving town soon. Who made it clear up front that he'd had enough of kids. She wanted only to raise her son, work and live a simple, quiet life.

"You know that and I know that," he said too softly for his brothers, now less than ten feet away, to hear. He nodded at them. "About time you two showed up."

They reached Emmy and Mac and stopped. And there she was, in the company of three big, brawny, very good-looking males, all with sky-blue eyes fringed in thick, dark lashes any woman would envy. Emmy certainly did. And she just about swooned.

Of the three, Mac clearly was the most attractive. His brothers were too young and their faces too smooth, whereas Mac had tiny crinkles at the corners of his eyes and the beginnings of brackets on either side his mouth. He seemed tougher and more seasoned, more *manly*. More everything that was appealing.

With a warning look at his brothers, Mac made the introductions. "Brian and Ian, meet Emmy Logan. She just moved here from Oakland and rents the cottage across the street."

At five-seven Emmy wasn't exactly short, and she was always battling ten extra pounds. Yet circled by these three men, each well over six feet, she felt petite and very feminine. Especially under their appreciative glances. Brian's and Ian's, that is. Mac's veiled eyes revealed nothing.

"Hello," she said, holding out her hand.

First Brian, whose hair was longer, then Ian, sporting a neat mustache and goatee, shook her hand. Both had firm grips and friendly expressions.

"How do you like the island?" Brian asked. A lock of dark, curly hair swooped over his forehead.

"It seems like a wonderful place," she said. "Pretty and quiet and friendly."

"You're right on the money." Ian flashed a toothy grin. "How long are you staying?"

"Forever. If all goes well."

"She has an eleven-year-old son," Mac said. "Jesse."

Emmy wished she knew what he was thinking, but his face was unreadable.

"I went to college with a Jesse," Ian said. "Good guy. This is a great place to grow up. Cleaner and safer than Oakland, for sure."

After winking at her, Brian nodded at Mac. "You seem to have found out a lot about Emmy."

"I was thinking the same thing." His twin chuckled. "What I'd like to know is—"

"There's nothing *to* know," Mac said, cutting him off. "Like I said, Emmy lives across the street. She stopped by to say hello. Period." He glared at them. Then he glared at Emmy.

Because that fierce, back-off look hurt—what had *she* done?—she glared back. Mac's face darkened before he glanced toward the gaping door of the van.

Brian and Ian guffawed as if they'd cracked a joke. Which only seemed to irritate Mac more. His jaw tightened.

Quickly sobering, both younger men shut their mouths. Their eyes, however, continued to twinkle. They didn't want to push their big brother too far, but neither were they cowed by him. It was obvious they loved and looked up to him.

Anyone could see he'd done a great job raising them. Emmy admired him for what he'd tackled at such an early age. And liked him all the more. From Mac's forbidding expression, he felt the complete opposite about her.

Now that she'd apologized to him and met his brothers, she'd leave them to their work and get started with hers. Aside from an occasional wave or nod, there was no reason to see or talk to any of them again.

Which would no doubt delight Mac and was fine with Emmy.

"If you need a kitchen to fix your lunch or a glass of water or anything at all, feel free to stop by," she said. She hadn't planned to offer, but any decent person would. For her neighborliness she earned a terse frown from Mac.

"No, thanks. We have what we need." He nodded at his brothers. "Ready to rock and roll?"

Without a "see you later" or "nice chatting with you" or "take care now," he began to pull tools from the van. If that wasn't a brush-off…

Refusing to let on that his brusqueness bothered her— and it did, a lot—she smiled sweetly at his brothers. "It was a pleasure meeting you both." When they returned the sentiment, she continued, "You're not rude like your brother. Maybe you can teach him some manners." Looking at Mac, she amped up her smile. "You have a terrific day. I know I will."

She turned away and without a backward glance strolled home to paint.

Chapter Three

Emmy had called him rude. Resisting the urge to stare dumbly after her, Mac leaned into the van and reached for the circular saw. Her door clicked open. Then firmly shut, the sound easy to hear in the silence that followed her killer exit.

A silence that seemed to mock him.

Well, he'd wanted to make his point, be sure she knew he wasn't about to start anything with her. Given the warmth he felt when she looked at him—hell, even when she didn't—he had to set her straight. Maybe himself, too.

By acting like a Neanderthal? Angry mostly at himself, Mac grabbed the saw and headed for the porch. He caught Brian staring at Emmy's door with a penetrating expression. Stroking his goatee, Ian, too, seemed deep in thought.

"What?" Mac growled.

"Guess she told *you*," Brian said, and damned if he wasn't grinning.

When Mac narrowed his eyes, Ian laughed. "You deserved it, too. You were a real butt. That's not the way you raised us."

"Nope," Brian said. "Makes me wonder why she set you off."

Because she got to him. Made him want to get to know her better when he had no business doing so. "We have work to do. Take this inside." He thrust the saw at Ian. "Brian, grab the rest of the stuff from the van."

Mac retrieved his tool belt from the passenger side of the van, buckled it on and followed his brothers up the front steps.

Hours later, after they tore off the back wall of the kitchen, hung and tacked down Visquine to keep out the cold—fat lot of good that did—Brian pushed his safety glasses to the top of his head, dropped his face mask and returned to the subject.

"At least explain why you were such a toad to Emmy."

"Yeah," Ian said.

They wouldn't move on until Mac answered the question. He pulled off his goggles, causing a shower of plasterboard flecks. "I'm leaving town in six weeks," he said. "There's a lot to do here, and I can't afford any distractions."

"And barking at her figures in how?" Ian asked. "You just met the woman. It's not like you're dating and she wants to get married or anything."

"She's a looker, and sweet, too. Maybe he *wants* to date her." Brian's lips curled knowingly, and Ian chuckled.

Mac rolled his eyes. "You're both full of sawdust. This is my time to be free, to travel and go to school, and I can't wait to leave. Unless either of you knuckle-heads wants to waste more time and drag this project out a few extra weeks?"

The teasing looks vanished.

"Not me." Brian donned his glasses and mask.

"Let's get back to work," Ian said.

Relieved, Mac picked up a crowbar and destroyed a kitchen cabinet.

IN THE BATHROOM of the cottage, Emmy returned Jesse's hairbrush, mousse and toothpaste, which he'd left on the counter, to his side of a medicine cabinet that had seen better days. Their new home was livable enough, but definitely needed updating and some TLC. Since Emmy had signed a year-long lease and they'd be here a while, she intended to do what she could to make the place comfortable and welcoming. In here that meant a new red shower curtain and matching bathroom rug.

She wiped down the counter and sink, chores she hadn't taken time for earlier. She'd been too eager to talk to Mac, a man she barely knew. Which wouldn't change, judging by his brusque manner. Emmy still felt the prick of his scowl and its implied message. *We're through here. Dismissed, over and out.* Her back stiffened.

The fact that he disliked her was no big deal. Perfect really, since she wasn't interested in him, either.

Which was a big, fat lie.

As she stood before the mirror and pulled her hair into a ponytail, she frowned into her own wistful eyes. "There'll be no more thinking about Mac Struthers today, Emmy Logan. He's a waste of energy, and you have work to do." And if she wanted to finish Jesse's room by three-thirty, a short timeline.

After quickly changing into a raggedy pink sweat-shirt and aging gray sweatpants, the perfect painting outfit, she carried the radio and a kitchen chair into

Jesse's room. The walls were a horrible baby-aspirin pink, unbearable for anyone, let alone an eleven-year-old boy. Thankfully the Rutherfords had given her the go-ahead to change the color to anything she wanted. At her expense.

Knowing she was going to paint in here, she and Jess had only unpacked the necessities—bedding and a few changes of clothes. The rest of his things were still in boxes stacked along the wall in the hallway.

Emmy found an oldies station on the radio. "Ain't No Sunshine" was playing—fitting for the gray day. Singing along, she covered the floor and bed with plastic tarp. She set down the two paint cans. Jesse had chosen a metallic blue for the ceiling, and a deeper, richer shade for the walls. The colors had to be custom-mixed and cost more than Emmy had budgeted. But pleasing her son, helping him feel good about this move, was more important than a few extra dollars. She'd compensate by waiting to paint the rest of the house until she'd collected a paycheck or two.

Within minutes she was standing on the chair, rolling a thick coat onto the ceiling. Grueling work that made her arms and neck hurt from reaching up. At least the room was small.

Still, covering the ceiling seemed to take forever. At last the job was done. Already the room looked brighter. Emmy stretched the kinks out of her back. A break would be nice, but it was almost noon and there was so much more to do. She managed to paint one wall before her empty stomach gurgled in protest.

"All right, all right," she muttered.

Time for lunch. Plus the fumes were awful. She wanted to open all the windows, but then, given the dampness and chilly outdoor temperature, the paint would never dry. The windows stayed shut.

Jess might have to use her room tonight. He'd need a good night's sleep so he wouldn't be tired in school. Meaning she'd be stuck with the cottage's lumpy living-room couch and was sure to wake up with a backache.

In the kitchen she washed her hands, then slapped together a peanut-butter-and-honey sandwich. She ate quickly. As she sponged off the table a knock sounded at the door.

Who could that be? *Mac?* It was shameful how hopeful she suddenly felt. He wasn't interested. And she shouldn't be, either.

There was no time to fix her face or her hair or change her clothes. Tugging down her sweatshirt and tightening her ponytail, she hurried to the door.

But instead of Mac, Brian stood on the stoop. Emmy hid her disappointment behind a friendly face. "Hello."

"Hi." Looking younger than twenty-two, his face streaked with grime, Brian smiled. "We had to shut off the water, and you said to come over if we needed anything…" He held up two liter-size empty bottles. "Would it be all right to fill these for me and Ian?"

Not Mac, too? Emmy wondered as she widened the door. "Of course. Come on in."

"Thanks." He wiped his boots on the mat, stepped inside and glanced around. From where he stood in the living room he easily took in the kitchen and hallway that led to Emmy's and Jesse's bedrooms.

"Nice little place." He sniffed. "I smell paint."

"That's because I'm painting Jesse's room. Right now it's pink." She wrinkled her nose.

"So you're changing it to blue?" Brian nodded at her

hair, and his mouth twitched. "Good color, but truthfully? I think you look better with light brown hair. You should wear a hat when you paint."

"Too late now." Emmy hadn't realized about her hair. She touched her crown, felt the stiff paint and laughed. "That's what happens when you roller the ceiling. Would you like a drink while I fill the bottles? By the way, all I have is tap water."

"No problem. Tap water sounds great, thanks."

Emmy took a glass from the newly papered cabinet shelf. "Does Mac know you're here?"

"He knows."

She filled the glass from the faucet. "Would you like to sit down?"

Looking regretful, Brian shook his head. "That'd be nice, but I can't stay that long."

Emmy didn't plan to say another word, but while Brian drank and she filled the empty bottles, she blurted out her thoughts.

"Mac doesn't seem to like me."

"He was nasty this morning, that's for sure." Brian wiped his mouth on the back of his hand. "If it helps any, Ian and I think you handled him just right."

He loaded the glass into the dishwasher, impressing Emmy. She really did need to teach Jess to do that. She liked Brian, who seemed a good deal warmer than his older brother.

"I don't appreciate being dismissed like some stray dog," she said.

"Believe me, I get that. The thing about Mac is, he's got a short time frame and a huge amount of work to do. Plus he tends to concentrate totally on the job. That focus is one reason why everybody in town wants to hire him and why he's stayed single."

This was interesting to know, but no excuse for the man's terse, abrupt manner. "I don't care how focused he is. He shouldn't treat anyone like that. You and Ian are so much friendlier. That counts for something, too. I'll bet that even after Mac leaves town, you'll bring in tons of business."

"We'll give it our best shot. The important thing is to keep the company going till he finishes school. That's what he wants."

With his voice expressionless and a face this side of gloomy, Brian seemed less than enthused. Emmy eyed him. "You don't really want to work in construction, do you?"

He shrugged. "I'm a media communications major. I'd rather go to grad school, earn my PhD and teach at a university."

"So do it and let Ian run the business."

"Not his thing, either. He's a computer geek. He's turned down job offers from Microsoft, Google and a couple of consulting companies. But hey, it's only for three years. Seeing the world is a longtime dream of Mac's. So is getting a college degree. Our parents were big on that. It's only fair he does it as a full-time student. After everything he did for us…"

Emmy didn't know Mac well, but she couldn't picture him forcing his brothers to run his business when they wanted other things. "If you tell him how you feel, I'm sure he'll understand," she said. "He'll find someone else to take over."

Brian shot her a panicked look. "Please, don't say anything."

"I won't," Emmy promised, turning off the tap. But never one to keep her opinions to herself, she voiced them. "I know that your parents died when you were young and that Mac raised you, so I understand why you feel indebted to him. That doesn't mean you should give up your dreams to work in his company. I can't imagine he'd want you to."

"He wouldn't." Brain screwed the tops onto the bottles. "That's why he'll never know."

Emmy frowned. "I'm confused."

"Let me explain. Mac gave up a full, four-year scholarship to take care of us."

"That's quite the sacrifice."

"He never talks about it. Back in high school he was something special, both a star tackle on the football team and a merit scholar. Everyone looked up to him—girls and guys and even the teachers. Half-a-dozen colleges offered him a free ride."

Given his size and muscular body, the athletic part wasn't surprising. That he was smart, too, only made him more appealing. "Wow," Emmy said. "That's impressive."

What a shame that he hadn't been able to take advantage of the educational opportunities offered him.

"His life before our parents' accident wasn't so hot, either," Brian went on. "Things were pretty tense. Mom and Dad were gone a lot. They both worked long hours at their jobs. When they *were* home at the same time, they mostly ragged on each other, and on us. For as long as I can remember, way before they died, Mac was the one who made sure Ian and I ate nutritious meals and wore clean clothes, stuff he taught himself. When we turned ten, he showed us how to cook and do the laundry, figuring we could do like he had and look after ourselves. He couldn't wait to graduate and leave home."

Emmy could see why. All that responsibility on a young kid's shoulders... As painful as her own childhood had been, she'd never had to worry about anyone else in the family. She couldn't even begin to imagine what Mac's life must have been like. Her heart ached for the little boy forced to grow up so quickly. Who'd never had the chance to enjoy his own childhood.

"I had no idea," she murmured.

"Now you know. He sacrificed a lot to keep us together. Ian and I will never forget that. We owe Mac big, and three years out of our lives is nothing." He gave Emmy a straight-on look. "If we had to, we'd die for him."

She had no doubt that was true. Despite hardships and pain, Mac was deeply loved. Which made him a very lucky man. Even if he was curt and unfriendly.

"Thank you for telling me," she said. "And don't worry, you can trust me to keep your secret."

"Figured I could."

"I'll take that as a compliment. Thank you."

"You're welcome." Brian grinned, then glanced at the wall clock. "Whoa, I've been here a while. I'd best get back before Mac comes looking for me. Thanks again for the water."

"I'm glad you stopped by." Liking this man very much, Emmy walked him to the door. "You're welcome here, so come back anytime. Ian, too. And...and Mac."

Not that he was off the hook. But the guy might need to use the bathroom or her sink.

"I'll pass that along. See you later, and good luck with the painting."

MAC LEANED OVER the porch and tossed a load of plasterboard into the Dumpster. The fine drizzle had stopped, but it sure was damp and cold. He grimaced. He wouldn't miss this weather. The school bus chugged to a stop in front of Emmy's. The door opened and Jesse hurried down the bus steps like a prison inmate heading for freedom. His jacket was tied around his waist and his backpack hung over one narrow shoulder. As the bus doors clapped shut, his back straightened and his chin jutted out.

A defensive pose that reminded Mac of the boy's mother the first day they'd met.

He'd thought about her surprising apology several times this morning. And how a short while later she'd put him in his place for his own brusque behavior. Which, after thinking it over, he realized he deserved. He felt pretty bad for acting like that.

His actions weighed on his mind the whole damn day, no thanks to Brian and Ian. They liked Emmy, and after Brian filled the water bottles at her place he'd yammered on and on about how cool she was. With all that, who could think about anything else?

As the bus pulled away, a few of the kids glanced through the windows. One pointed and laughed at Jesse, cruel actions that had Mac stiffening. The boy gave no indication of noticing, just stood tall and slid his eyes to the black stripes on the side of the vehicle.

The second the bus rounded the curve, his shoulders slumped. He kicked a rock, sending it and a clump of mud flying. By the looks of things, his first day at school had been a hell of a rough one.

Though Mac had never experienced the horror of kids laughing at him, he knew that carrying the weight of the world on your back was no fun. He felt for the boy.

"Hey, Jesse," he called out. "How you doin'?"

Apparently Jesse hadn't noticed him before, for he glanced toward Mac with a surprised expression. "Hey, Mac."

At that moment Ian and Brian tromped through the front door, carrying a pile of trash between them.

"You're Jesse, right?" Ian said as he and Brian sidled toward the porch railing.

"How'd you know my name?"

His biceps bulging with effort, Brian grunted a reply. "Your mom told us about you." He didn't speak again until he and Ian had hefted their load into the Dumpster. "I saw the new color for your bedroom ceiling," he said, wiping his palms on the thighs of his jeans. "Reminds me of a summer sky in the afternoon. Real nice."

"Uh, okay."

Jesse looked wary, and no wonder. He had no idea who he was talking to.

"Don't mind these two jokers," Mac said as he moved down the steps. "They're my kid brothers, Ian and Brian."

The boy's eyes rounded. "You guys are twins, right?"

Both brothers laughed and followed Mac down the steps.

"Identical, but we try to make it easy on people." Brian touched the hair brushing his collar. "That's why I wear my hair long."

"And why I grew a mustache and goatee," Ian said. "And also because I'm a computer geek—when I'm not building kitchens."

"Cool." Jesse turned his attention to the Dumpster. "Wow, you guys put a lot of garbage in there."

"We've been at it since first thing this morning, and we're not done yet," Mac said. "Ripping out the back of the kitchen and stripping the ceiling and other walls down to nothing but the framing takes time. And hard work." He rubbed the small of his back, which ached.

"What's framing?"

"The beams and such that hold up the walls and roof," Brian said.

Ian nodded. "Like the bones in your body support you."

"Can I see it?" Jesse asked.

Mac didn't see why not. "Sure."

As the boy deposited his backpack and jacket on the wet ground, Emmy's door opened. In baggy, old clothes, her hair in a ponytail and a blue smear on one cheek, she looked cute. Her quick, unsmiling glance at Mac doubled his guilt for treating her so coolly this morning.

"Jesse, hi!" She hurried forward, as if anxious to be near him. "Where are you going?"

"Mac said I could see Mr. and Mrs. Rutherford's kitchen. He and his brothers took down the walls and ceiling and stuff. They're gonna show me the framing. It's kind of like your bones."

The kid actually sounded excited. Mac figured Emmy'd be happy about that. Wrong. She frowned.

"But I haven't seen you all day," she said, plucking his backpack and jacket from the ground and brushing them off. "You're always hungry after school. You need a snack, and I'm anxious to hear about your day. And wait'll you see your room! I'm almost finished, and the colors look great."

She was painfully eager to shower her son with attention, and Jesse looked embarrassed by it.

"I don't want to right now. I want to see what Mac and his brothers are doing."

"Oh." Emmy's face fell. "Of course."

Her son had hurt her without even realizing it. Kids

could be so thoughtless. Jesse had no idea how lucky he was to have a mother who loved him, who wanted to spend time with him and cared about his day.

Mac hated to see Emmy so downhearted. Here was his chance to atone for his earlier sins. As Jesse turned his back on her and started toward Mac, he gestured for the boy to stop. "You go have that snack, talk to your mom and check out your new room. Then come over."

"Do I have to?" Jesse asked, rolling his eyes.

Mac nodded. "We're here another hour or so today, and nearly every day for the next six weeks. There's plenty of time to see the kitchen."

"Okay." The boy exhaled loudly. "If I have to."

All Mac had done was ask Emmy's son to spend a little while with her, but she gave him a grateful smile, a smile that warmed him. She'd forgiven him and he felt like a million bucks.

That bothered him big-time because despite thinking about Emmy most of the day, he'd almost convinced himself that he wasn't interested in her, that she was on his mind because his brothers kept dropping her name.

Now he knew he'd been fooling himself. He liked Emmy Logan. All too much.

Chapter Four

Tuesday morning Jesse dragged himself into the kitchen wearing yet another Street Kings T-shirt, the same baggy jeans and sneakers as yesterday—sadly, the school had not sent a note home asking him to wear nicer clothes—and a hostile expression as familiar as the gelled-down cowlick at the crown of his head.

And he'd been in such high spirits at bedtime last night, his mood propelled by the hour he'd spent with Mac and his brothers. Jesse'd come home animated and happy, his lightheartedness so like the child he was before his father had walked away and he'd forgotten how to laugh. Yes, he'd still balked at helping with the dinner dishes and had fought bedtime, but his upbeat attitude persisted.

Emmy had prayed it lasted, but this morning her son was his normal glum self. Which added an invisible load to her shoulders, a burden born of worry and concern. And her own fatigue. Thanks to a miserable night on the lumpy sofa, while Jesse slept in her bed, she wasn't in the best humor, either.

Tired and grumpy as she felt, she wanted to coax back Jesse's good mood, start his day on a cheerful note. "Good morning, sleepyhead," she said, smiling.

"Morning."

She handed him his orange juice and he sat down at the table. Emmy freshened her coffee, then joined him.

When he drained his glass and stared broodingly into space, she slid the cereal box toward him. "You'd better eat while you have time."

His mouth tightened. "I'm not going to school today."

And wasn't this an instant replay of yesterday? Would tomorrow be the same, and the next day and the next? Emmy fervently hoped not. "You're going," she said. "Period."

"But I could help unpack boxes and put up the posters in my room. You said the paint fumes should be gone now, and you want me to help."

Looking forward to sleeping in her own bed tonight, Emmy nodded. "I do, and you will, this evening. Now, eat."

Jesse filled his bowl. Instead of wolfing down his breakfast as he had the day before, this morning he ate little. The air was heavy with his melancholy. He hadn't enjoyed his first day at school and clearly dreaded the second.

Stomach tight with anxiety, Emmy touched his tense forearm. "Moving to a new town and new school isn't easy. You've only been once. Give it time."

Jess batted her hand away. "Time won't help. I hate it here."

"If you'll just *try,* Jesse—"

"I don't want to talk about it!" He glared at her, then glued his eyes to the back of the cereal box. Shutting her out.

By now she should be used to the hostile silences, but they always stung. Especially when he was hurting and needed her. Couldn't he see that she was here for him and always would be, no matter what?

Refusing to give up, Emmy tried again. "Once you get the hang of things and make friends, I know you'll feel differently."

"What friends?" Her son curled his lip. "Nobody here likes me. They're all lame, anyway."

Words that pained her deeply. "When they get to know you, they'll love you just as I do. You'll see."

A yearning look filled Jesse's face, gone in a blink. His expression darkened. "I wish I was back in Oakland. Why'd you do this to me, Mom?"

"You know why!" Emmy heard her voice rise and snapped her mouth shut. Getting mad wouldn't help matters. After a deep, calming breath, she continued in a normal, reasonable tone. "I've told you before, we're not going back—ever. So put the idea out of your mind for good. Now, tell me about Mrs. Hatcher. Is she as nice as people say?"

She'd asked the same question after school yesterday. In a hurry to join Mac across the road, Jess had merely shrugged. Later, afraid of taking his smile away, Emmy had steered clear of mentioning school.

"She's okay."

With his head bent over his cereal, Emmy couldn't see his eyes. "I can't wait to meet her this afternoon," she said, hoping this would elicit some information.

Now her son looked up with a stricken expression. "You're not going to tell her what I said about the kids at school, are you?"

"I don't know," Emmy said. "The subject may come up."

"Aw, geez." Jesse cringed. "I don't have to be there when you talk to her, do I?"

Wanting this first meeting to be just her and Mrs. Hatcher, Emmy shook her head. "You can wait for me in the school library and we'll ride home together."

His spoon clattered against the bowl. "I don't want to ride with you, and I don't want to go to school." When Emmy set her jaw, Jesse quickly added, "But since you're making me, I'll take the bus back and wait for you here."

His challenging look made her want to scream. Working to remain calm, she attempted to reason with him. "You know I can't leave you alone, Jess. Who'd look after you?"

"I'm eleven years old. I don't need a babysitter."

Yet another battle that had begun with Tyrell. Having been on his own for years, the sixteen-year-old Street Kings leader thought Jesse should be, too. He also thought Jesse should own a gun. Emmy shuddered.

"I know how to pour myself a glass of milk and make a sandwich," her son said. "I know how to use the phone if there's an emergency. I'll be fine by myself."

Even if the snack part was true, Emmy wasn't sure about the rest. She was about to explain for the hundredth time that no, she didn't believe he was quite ready yet, when he brightened.

"I know. I'll go to the Rutherfords'. Today Mac and his brothers are framing in the new back wall of the kitchen, putting in the insulation and a bunch of other cool stuff."

Mac and his brothers this, Mac and his brothers that. Since yesterday afternoon, Jesse had talked about them almost nonstop. He seemed to really like them. Emmy understood. She liked them, too—especially Mac. But only because he was nice to Jesse.

While she was grateful to the Struthers men for making her son feel welcome and pleased that he liked these positive role models, she worried they might not want him hanging around when they were busy.

"You can't just go over there, Jess. They have a lot to do, and you might get in the way."

"I didn't yesterday. They even let me help carry trash to the Dumpster."

"That's great, but I'm not sure how long I'll be gone. What if they want to leave before I get back from talking with Mrs. Hatcher?"

"Then like I said, I'll wait for you here. Please, Mom, don't make me sit in the school library."

While she silently debated whether or not to let Jesse stay here alone, he shoved his chair back and stood.

"What do you think I'll do, call Tyrell? I said I wouldn't."

He met her gaze directly and she believed him. He didn't give her a chance to say so.

"You don't trust me!"

Wasn't this type of drama supposed to happen with teenagers? Jess was barely a tween, but if his outburst was any indication of the future… *Lord, grant me strength.*

Yet the truth was, she *didn't* trust her son. Even if he wouldn't phone Tyrell, his judgments weren't the best. Just look at what had happened in Oakland. Emmy didn't want to get into this, not a scant twenty minutes before the bus was due. So she gave him another valid reason.

"You know what a worrywart I am. I'm just not ready for you to look after yourself."

"You'd better get ready, Mom. Because I'm growing up."

Emmy sighed. "I know." A glance at the clock and she, too, stood. "It's late. Better hurry in the bathroom, but put your dishes in the dishwasher first."

"I'll do that after I brush my teeth."

Of course he didn't, simply pocketed his lunch money, grabbed his jacket and left. No kiss, either.

"I'll look for you in the school library," she reminded him.

Giving no indication he heard, Jesse slammed the door behind him. Whether from fatigue or hormones— her period was about to start—or worry over her son, Emmy felt like crying.

Jesse was lonely. He needed a friend, anyone could see that. A scary thought entered her mind. What if he found a gang here and started hanging out with them? As quiet and friendly as Halo Island was, no town was without its troublemakers.

Chilled, she hoped that he made a friend soon—God willing, a nice, normal boy—and began to enjoy school.

As she had yesterday, she stood in the living room and peeked through the space between the drapes. What she saw made her heart ache. Jesse's face was grim, his shoulders hunched and his hands stuffed into his jeans pockets. He looked miserable.

Her protective maternal instincts kicked in. She longed to run outside and fold him in a loving hug. But Jesse wouldn't like that.

Lately he didn't seem to like *her*. Was that normal? Regardless, it cut deeply. Emmy wished she had a friend here to confide in, someone to give her perspective.

In that way, she wasn't so different from her son. They were both alone and lonely in this new place. Tears filled her eyes and trickled freely down her face. "Stop feeling sorry for yourself," she scolded, swiping at her cheeks. "You'll make friends when you start work."

She pulled a clean tissue from the pocket of her jeans and blew her nose. A few minutes later, the bus picked up Jesse. For some reason, watching him climb the steps cheered her up a little. Not enough to stop the tears, though. She was still standing in front of the window, sniffling and struggling to get hold of herself, when Mac's van pulled to a stop in front of the Rutherfords' house.

Now *that* stopped the tears. Her heart gave a funny little leap. Emmy compressed her lips. She so did not want to care about Mac. And even if she owed him for putting the light back into Jesse's eyes for a few hours yesterday, she was still mad at him and not about to thank him. She didn't intend to speak to him at all today.

Risk another brush-off? No, thank you.

Too much to do, anyway. With boxes still to unpack, pictures to hang and a casserole to prepare before this afternoon's meeting with Mrs. Hatcher, she was far too busy for Mac Struthers.

So when he slid out of the driver's seat and glanced at the cottage, Emmy backed away from the window. As she turned toward the kitchen, the phone rang.

EMMY WAS LOOKING at him. Mac sensed her gaze as surely as he felt the slap of the cold morning air. He squinted at her living-room window, but with only a crack in the drapes and darkness beyond, he couldn't see her.

Who knew if she really was watching him? Might be his imagination. Just in case, though, he nodded a hello. He wished she'd come out like she had yesterday, but he also hoped she wouldn't. He couldn't stop thinking about her, and it was best for both of them if she stayed away.

Her lonely son weighed on his mind, too. The way he'd followed Mac like a puppy. The kid wasn't bad, just needed some male attention and guidance. A job Mac wasn't about to take on. Been there, done that. Once he finished this remodel, he was a free man, tied to no one.

Switching his attention away from Emmy and her son, he took the porch steps two at a time, crossed the wood planking and knocked on the Rutherfords' door.

Tom opened it without his usual smile.

"Morning." Mac wiped his feet and stepped inside, closing the door behind him.

Everything in the living room was covered with protective plastic and a fine layer of dust from yesterday's demolition. The two heaters Mac and his brothers had set up were running, but with only the Visquine separating the kitchen from the great outdoors, the inside temperature was way below normal. Tom was bundled up in thick sweaters. There was no sign of Melinda. Unlike yesterday the couple seemed in no hurry to leave.

Mac noted the older man's solemn expression. "Hope you and Melinda weren't too cold last night. Once we finish clearing out the debris this morning, we'll put up the framework for the new back wall and add the insulation. That'll help some, and once we install the new thermal windows, this place will be toasty warm."

"We shut our bedroom door and cozied under a down comforter, so we slept fine."

"The water will be off for a few more days," Mac said. "You might be more comfortable at a motel."

"We won't be needing that, not with what's happened." Tom scratched the back of his neck. "Something came up. Melinda's calling Emmy now."

Phone in hand, Tom's wife appeared from the hallway and waved without smiling. Wondering what the deal was, Mac listened to her end of the call.

"I wasn't sure if you were dressed at this hour," she said. "Otherwise, I'd have run over there." She paused, listening.

In the brief gap of silence Mac wondered what Emmy slept in. With a son in the house, probably nothing revealing. Flannel pajamas? An oversize T-shirt? Now *that* appealed to him, and he pictured her in a man's shirt that hung to mid-thigh and slipped off one shoulder. Her long legs bare, her breasts unbound and the little points where the cotton brushed her nipples. From there it was only a simple jump of the imagination to picture her pulling the shirt over her head…

Mac swallowed and hoped to God his groin behaved. A surefire way to make certain of that was to stop fantasizing about Emmy Logan and focus on Melinda, who stared solemnly at the floor.

"Could you stop by for a minute?" she said into the phone. An instant later she disconnected. "Emmy will be right over."

Emmy, coming here? *Now?* Mac dreaded seeing her. He was also more than curious. What was going on, and why did it involve both him and Emmy? Soon enough, he'd know.

Seconds later as he stood in the shadows to the side of the door, Emmy knocked. Tom greeted her, and she entered the house breathless and pink-cheeked from the cold. No lipstick. Her hair was tucked behind her ears.

Nothing suggestive or seductive in those faded jeans

and short, wool jacket. Yet Mac's heart thunked harder in his chest than it had any right to.

What was it about this woman that had him feeling like a kid with a major crush?

Her gaze collided with his, then darted away. Not before he noted her red-rimmed eyes. Anyone could see she'd been crying.

If there was one thing that rattled him, it was a crying woman. Had Jesse hurt her again? If so, Mac would… *Stay out of it.* Their problems were none of his business, and he wasn't about to get involved. Yeah, but he still wanted to know.

"Look at this place," Emmy said to the room as a whole. "Now I understand what Jess was talking about. It's certainly…interesting in here." She shoved her hands in her coat pockets. "And freezing."

"We don't mind the cold or the mess or living without running water," Tom said. "Because we know the result will be worth the dust and inconvenience."

Mac nodded. "Guaranteed."

Emmy's lips thinned. She wouldn't look at him. After her warm, grateful smile yesterday afternoon, this puzzled him. That and those teary eyes.

"We'd invite you both to sit down and offer you coffee, but…" Melinda made a helpless gesture at the chaotic room.

"That's okay." Emmy turned her back on Mac. "What's up?"

"We just got a call from Valley Hospital in Ellensburg. That's in central Washington, where Melinda grew up." Tom placed a hand on his wife's shoulder. "Early this morning, her uncle Mort suffered a massive heart attack."

Melinda's eyes filled. "He's almost ninety, the last of

his generation on my side of the family. Tom and I are all he has left, and we love him so…" Fiddling with a much-used tissue, she went silent.

"We're catching the ten-ten ferry," Tom continued in a grave voice. "Then driving on to Ellensburg. We'll be gone at least a week, maybe longer."

"What with the kitchen torn apart this is a good time to go." Melinda dabbed her eyes and tried to smile. "I just wish it wasn't for such an awful reason."

Tom glanced at the floor and cleared his throat.

Great, now *they* were crying. At least Mac knew how to deal with grief. "I'm real sorry," he said.

Emmy turned toward him, and for about a second held his gaze. Her eyes were filled with sympathy and shiny with unshed tears. She'd damn well better hold it together. Mac tensed.

"That's a shame," she said before she gulped and looked away.

Caught up in their own wrenching emotions, the Rutherfords didn't appear to notice Emmy grasping for control. After a moment during which Mac sucked in his breath, she visibly pulled herself together.

"What would you like me to do?"

She sounded okay now, calm. *Phew.* Mac exhaled.

"If you'd keep the house key and unlock the door for Mac in the morning and dead-bolt it after he leaves at night, we'd appreciate it. It locks by itself, but not the dead bolt. And maybe you could check on the house this weekend to make sure everything's okay. In return, we'll waive a month's rent."

"You don't have to do that. I'm only across the road, and it's really no trouble at all. Nothing a decent neighbor wouldn't do."

"And we appreciate that," Tom said. "But we've made up our minds. You're painting the inside of the cottage on your own dime. You're a single mom and haven't even started your new job, and you came a long way to get here. Since you've already paid for this month, you can skip the next one."

"If you're sure." Emmy bit her lip. "That's so nice of you. Thanks."

Her face was as easy to read as a level, and Mac saw the gratitude. She must be broke, or close to it. Was that the reason for the tears? With women, you never knew. And damn it, he didn't care.

Until a thought hit him. What if she was crying because of *him?* Could be, since she wouldn't look at him and tensed whenever he spoke. After all, he *had* been a rude jackass yesterday morning. Maybe he'd misinterpreted that smile yesterday afternoon.

Well, hell. He could feel her deliberately not looking at him. Yep, that had to be it. *Double hell.*

"No, Emmy, thank *you*," Tom said. "You've only been here a few days and we already feel close to you. Couldn't have picked a better neighbor if we'd tried."

Melinda managed a fleeting smile at Emmy before turning to Mac. "We've been over the kitchen plans with you numerous times, and you know exactly what we want. But if you—either of you—have questions about anything, don't hesitate to call. We'll keep our cell phones on."

Mac nodded. The Rutherfords' bad news aside, their being gone meant he could work later at night and on Saturday. With any luck he'd finish the job early.

Trouble was, he and Emmy would see each other every morning and probably every night. Worse, he'd be thinking about her all the time. Now, with her upset at him…it wouldn't be pleasant. Hopefully she'd get over it. If not, he wasn't sure what he'd do.

Six weeks and he was out of here. The days couldn't go by fast enough.

STANDING ON the half-stripped floor just before noon, Ian squinted at Mac. "You've been in a bum mood all morning. If you wanted a key to this place, why didn't you just ask the Rutherfords?"

Mac had thought about doing exactly that. Sure would've made things easier. "Because they're giving Emmy a month's free rent to lock and unlock the door for us, and she needs the money."

By the surprised look on both brothers' faces, the words had come out more harshly than intended.

"What *is* your problem?" Brian squinted at him through his safety glasses. "No, let me guess. Emmy's barely speaking to you and that bugs the hell out of you."

Mac nudged the toe of his boot under a square of blue linoleum yet to be removed. "How'd you know that?"

"What'd I tell ya?" Brian said, trading looks with Ian.

"You were a jerk yesterday morning," Ian said. "You need to apologize."

"Hey, I showed Jesse around for over an hour yesterday. She appreciated that—I saw it on her face." Her forgiving smile was still burned into his brain.

"And that's good," Brian said. "But not the same as an actual apology. *I'm sorry I was an ass.* She needs to hear those words.

While Mac thought that over, Ian's stomach growled loudly. "I'm gonna die if I don't eat soon. Think I'll head for Island Burgers and pick us up some lunch." He glanced at Brian and Mac. "What do you two want?"

"For starters, I could use some air and I want to check my e-mail," Ian said with a pointed look Mac's way. "I'll go with you."

Mac slid his wallet from his hip pocket and handed Brian a bill. "Bring me a double cheeseburger, fries and a pop."

"Will do. Maybe when we come back you'll be in a better mood."

"There's only one way that'll happen," Ian said. "Walk over to Emmy's and say you're sorry."

Chapter Five

Emmy had cried on and off all morning. PMS, she decided as she stood sniffling at the sink at noon, washing the pots and pans she'd dirtied while making tonight's casserole. That, and anxieties about Jesse, the Rutherfords' sad news, the gloomy, gray day. And Mac. He'd been decent enough earlier at Tom and Melinda's, but that didn't compensate for his unsmiling expression and harsh tone yesterday morning. Infuriating man!

Certainly no reason to cry. Yet here she was, leaking more tears. She sniffled then set her jaw. Hormones or not, she was sick and tired of this pity party, which would get her nowhere. Plus if she wanted to look halfway decent for her appointment with Jesse's teacher—in other words, no red eyes or stuffy nose—she'd better cheer up now.

She pulled the drain plug. "The crying will stop now," she announced over the water gurgling down the drain.

Without even drying her hands she marched into the bathroom, splashed cold water on her face and blotted her face dry with a towel. She blew her nose. There, that was better. Even if she did still look a wreck.

She was reaching for eye makeup and foundation, a girl's best allies, when someone knocked at the door.

Oh, great. Well, it *was* lunchtime. Probably Brian or Ian, or both, come to get water or wash their hands. She hadn't seen either of them today.

Looking forward to their friendly company, she raked her hair with a comb, which given her puffy eyes, didn't help much. She'd say she was suffering from allergies.

She headed for the door. Pasted a smile on her face and opened it. To her surprise, Mac stood there. The sleeves of his grimy blue workshirt were rolled halfway up his thick forearms, and his hair stood up in places, as if he'd run his hand through it. Against the gray noon light his eyes looked especially blue.

No man had the right to be so ruggedly handsome and compelling, not when Emmy was mad at him. Her heart lifted and a dreamy sigh slipped out. Dismayed, she eyed him. "Yes?"

"Uh, hi," he said, his breath cloudy in the frigid air. He shoved his hands into his jeans pockets. "Mind if I come in?"

The way she felt right now, lonely, vulnerable and aching, allowing Mac into her home was dangerous. Wishing his brothers were with him so she'd feel safer, Emmy peered around him. The black truck was nowhere in sight.

"Where are Ian and Brian?"

"Out picking up lunch." Mac stamped his feet and rubbed his arms. "It's cold out here."

Of course the man was coatless. That, his pleading look and the fact that Emmy *had* offered the use of her sink, convinced her to let him in.

Carefully standing out of his way, she opened the door wide. Mac wiped his feet, then crossed the threshold. The living room seemed even smaller now.

"The bathroom's down the hall," she said, closing the door behind him. Recalling that she'd left makeup on the counter, she quickly added, "It's a little messy in there, so if you'll wait just a minute I'll run and straighten up."

"Don't bother. I don't need the bathroom."

"You want a glass of water then," she guessed.

Mac shook his head.

"Okay, then exactly why *are* you here?"

"I…"

Studying the carpet and shifting his weight, he seemed ill at ease. Well, so was she. She crossed her arms.

"Hell, I may as well just come out and say it. I acted like a jerk yesterday morning. I owe you an apology."

Emmy hadn't expected this. Mac's genuine regret snuffed out her anger. She uncrossed her arms. "That's very sweet. Thank you."

A look of pure relief filled his face, at odds with his terse nod and failure to meet her eyes. The man was clearly uncomfortable. Because he'd apologized, or because she'd called him sweet?

"That's two apologies in as many days, one from each of us," she said. "I guess we're even now."

"I guess we are."

His lips flirted with a smile, then widened into a charming grin that crinkled his eyes. Warmth that transformed him from handsome to irresistible. Emmy's heart felt pounds lighter.

She meant to smile back. Instead, to her horror, fresh tears filled her eyes and a sob clogged her throat.

Instantly Mac sobered. "You were crying this morning, too." He looked confused. "Shi— Shoot. What else did I do wrong?"

The man *would* think her tears were about him. "This has nothing at all to do with you," she stated, swiping furiously at her cheeks. "And I'm not crying."

Now he looked panicky. "Yes, you are. Please don't."

"I said I wasn't. It's allergies." So that he'd stop scrutinizing her, Emmy pivoted away from him and blinked hard. "Are you sure you don't want something to drink?" she asked, pleased that she sounded normal and not like a blubbering fool. "A glass of water or a cup of coffee? I made it this morning, but I'm happy to heat it in the microwave."

Why had she offered? She didn't want Mac here, not when she felt so raw.

"Coffee sounds good."

He followed her into the kitchen and sat down. The big man dwarfed the little table. He took one of the chairs she and Jess didn't use, as if he somehow knew their places. Emmy pulled two mugs from the cabinet and filled them. While the microwave worked its magic, she set out milk and sugar. She carried the steaming coffees to the table, then sat down across from Mac.

What to chat about that wouldn't set off the tears? "It sure is cold today," she said.

"No rain, though. That's a nice change."

"Yes, it is."

Emmy sipped coffee and searched her mind for another safe topic of conversation. "What a shame about Melinda's uncle."

"Yeah. You never know, though, he may be okay."

"I hope so." To her dismay, her eyes flooded again.

Mac drew his brows together and studied his coffee for several long moments. "I'll probably regret this, but maybe you should tell me what's got you so upset."

She didn't want to burden anyone with her troubles, let alone this man. But they tumbled out, anyway. "The move has been really hard. Jesse's so unhappy, and we're fighting more than ever." She tried to smile without success. "You wouldn't know it, but he used to be a really sweet little guy. Yesterday after he came back from visiting you and your brothers, he was my excited boy again. Well, almost. But it didn't last. This morning was awful." Afraid she'd break down, she smoothed her thumb over a nick in the tabletop. "I don't know what to do."

"Now there's a subject I'm an expert at," Mac said in a soothing voice Emmy had never heard. "With boys Jesse's age, mood changes come with the territory."

If anyone knew that, Mac did, and his words helped. Emmy continued. "It got worse when he started hanging around with those gang members. Jess doesn't like it here. He wants to go back to Oakland. I keep telling him he'll change his mind and grow to like Halo Island, but the truth is, I don't know if he will. You've seen how stubborn he is." She bit her lip. "What if he doesn't make any friends? What if he always hates the island and his school?" She swallowed. "What if he finds a gang here?"

"As far as I know, we don't have any on the island," Mac said. "Give Jesse time. He'll come around."

Hadn't she said more or less the same thing to herself? "I'll try."

"That's all you can do." Mac sat back.

A more comfortable silence followed.

"Thanks for letting me talk about this," she said. "It's… I appreciate your listening."

"Sure thing." His eyes were filled with understanding, probably because he knew exactly what she was going through. "Jesse needs a man's guidance—a man who sticks around."

"Do men like that exist?" She managed a laugh. "Because I sure haven't met one." She'd certainly abandoned her hopes and dreams on that score.

"You're a beautiful woman. The right man will find you and your son."

Emmy didn't believe him.

"Trust me on that," Mac said as if he'd read her thoughts. "What else is on your mind?"

His compassion and willingness to listen coaxed her to share her deepest doubts. "Jesse's had such a rough time. Sometimes...sometimes I wonder about my mothering skills," she admitted in a voice so soft, she wasn't sure he even heard it.

Ashamed, she glanced at her hands, tightly wrapped around her mug even though the heat almost burned her skin.

"Hey." Mac reached across the table and clasped her wrist.

Without knowing how it happened, she was on her feet, standing in the warm circle of his arms. Crying her heart out and absorbing his warmth while he rubbed her back and murmured softly. It had been such a long time since someone had held her like that. Mac's chest was solid and broad, and he smelled of sawdust and man. His quiet strength comforted her, and after a while she pulled a tissue from her pocket and blew her nose.

"I keep crying and wish I'd stop," she said. "It's embarrassing."

"Emmy, look at me." Mac gently nudged up her chin

until she met his eyes. "You're a good mother, and Jess is a good kid. Moving is tough. Exhausting. You're in a rough patch right now, that's all."

"Do you really think so?"

He nodded. "Things will get better. I promise."

He looked at her straight on, and she believed him. "Thanks for the vote of confidence."

"Anytime."

He didn't release her and she didn't pull away. Her palms slid to his chest, resting in the slight hollows beneath his shoulders. Tension, powerful and undefined, bloomed in the air, and everything shifted. Mac's eyes darkened in awareness.

Emmy's nerves began to thrum. "Mac? What's happening here?"

"Then you feel it, too." His thumb stroked her cheek. "This heat between us."

Unable to speak, captivated by the caress of his thumb and the pull of those blue eyes, she nodded.

"What I'm feeling—it's dangerous."

And impossible to fight. Wanting, needing his lips against hers, Emmy rose on her toes and looped her arms around his neck.

"Emmy…" he warned, and started to untangle her arms.

"Don't. Just kiss me."

MAC GAZED into the eyes of the warm, vibrant woman in his arms. He hadn't held a woman in so long. She smelled lemony and sweet, and the press of her soft curves against his body felt so damned good.

He'd wanted this, wanted to kiss her since they'd first met. Problem was, she was lonely and emotional and likely looking for more than he could give. Kissing her meant trouble he hadn't the time for.

Mustering control, he forced himself away from that tempting mouth. "This is *not* a good idea."

"I couldn't agree more."

She stretched up and brushed her lips across his. Her eyes drifted shut. His body jumped to life, and he forgot that this was wrong, forgot everything but the willing woman in his arms.

Groaning, he captured her mouth for more. Quickly deepened contact, coaxing her lips open and tangling his tongue with hers. He tasted coffee, salt from her tears and need, all of it fueling his hunger, which flared so fierce and raging his knees almost buckled.

He wanted more, wanted to kiss her until she forgot her worries, forgot everything but him and the pleasure between them. Need surged through him to back her to the sofa, lay her down and bury himself in her feminine sweetness. Somewhere in the dim recesses of his brain, he remembered. Loving Emmy this way would only lead to complications he didn't want and couldn't afford.

Apprehensive, he broke the kiss, let her go and stepped away, his breathing as labored as if he'd run up the Rutherfords' steps with a load of cement. "This can't happen. I'm leaving soon," he said, though she already knew that. "I can't get involved."

"I don't want anything from you, Mac. I just… I needed to be held."

So she said, but the look on her face—desire and longing and tenderness—scared him spitless.

At that moment he heard male laughter. It sounded very close. The living-room drapes were wide-open.

Could anyone see into the kitchen? Mac hoped to God not. He swore.

"My brothers are here," he muttered an instant before they knocked.

"Don't worry, they'll never know what just happened." Emmy walked briskly toward the door, smoothing down her sweater and her hair. "Hello there," she said, sounding like her usual, friendly self.

Mac silently applauded her great acting.

"We came to wash up and get Mac," Ian said.

"Please come in."

Mac didn't care much for the way Ian and Brian scrutinized Emmy, whose lips were pink and kiss-swollen. Tensing, he narrowed his eyes in warning.

When neither of them said a word, he relaxed. Smart guys, his kid brothers.

They kidded around and made small talk with Emmy while they all washed up. Not about to stay here a second longer, Mac rinsed and dried his hands and headed for the door with a nod. "Thanks, and see you."

A CRYING JAG, melting kisses with Mac and now talking with Jesse's new teacher made for an emotional roller coaster of a day. Yet by the time Emmy's conference with Liza Hatcher ended, she felt more hopeful and positive than she had in a long time. Jesse's pretty teacher was as nice as people claimed, a woman who clearly loved children. Colorful posters and students' projects decorated her classroom, conveying both warmth and nurturing.

On top of that, Emmy liked her as a person. They were about the same age, and she thought they might become friends. Especially after Liza invited her to the monthly Saturday-night bunco game at the Halo Island Community Center.

"If you come, you'll meet some of the terrific women who live on the island," she said. "I'll introduce you around."

Emmy thought that sounded like fun, but with no one to watch Jesse… "I'd love to, but I doubt I'll make it this time. Once Jess makes friends and has a place to go for the evening, I'll definitely be there."

"Great." Liza smiled, pushed back her chair and rose.

Emmy, who sat across the wonderfully cluttered desk, also stood. "Thank you for meeting with me today."

"I'm so glad we did, and I appreciate your candor. Jesse's school files are full of information, but talking with you filled in the gaps. It's good to know about his brush with gang life. I'll do what I can to help him feel comfortable and welcome."

Emmy had no doubt of that. Like Mac, Liza had said there were no gangs on the island, which was a huge relief. "I appreciate that. Do his clothes bother you?" she asked as Liza walked her to the door.

"Not at all. We don't have a dress code. I've lived on the island most of my life, so if there's anything you want to know, or if you need to check on Jesse's progress, don't hesitate to call me—even at home."

"Thanks. I will. He's waiting for me in the library. How do I get there?"

"Turn left at the end of the hall. Second door on the right. You can't miss it."

Ten minutes later, with her son buckled into the passenger seat and inhaling the granola bar Emmy had brought him, she pulled out of the mostly deserted school parking lot. The winter sunset came early in the

Pacific Northwest, and at four-thirty darkness had almost fallen. At least it wasn't raining.

"I like Mrs. Hatcher," Emmy said. "She said good things about you. She thinks you're very bright and that you'll do well in her class."

"She said that?" Jesse looked pleased.

"She did," Emmy said, smiling.

He was quiet for a moment, then nodded at the fog swirling around them. "Mrs. Hatcher says the fog sometimes makes a ring over the ocean that looks like a halo. That's how the island got its name."

"I didn't know that. Interesting."

This was their second easy conversation in two days. Emmy hoped Jesse's good mood lasted. "I hung all the pictures today," she said. "And right after you left this morning, Mrs. Rutherford called. Her uncle had a heart attack. He lives in another town, and she and Mr. Rutherford have gone to take care of him. They'll be away at least a week. They gave me their house key. I'll be letting Mac and his brothers in every day and locking up after they leave."

"Oh."

While Jess polished off the last of his granola bar and stared out the window, Emmy thought about Mac. Now that she'd kissed him, the idea of seeing him twice a day sent a rush of pleasure through her. She tried not to remember how she'd cried on him, then shamelessly begged him to kiss her, only concentrating on the lovely kisses that had followed. Her lips still tingled from his thorough and avid attention.

Mac Struthers was good at more than remodeling houses. Did he make love with the same intensity? She wouldn't mind finding out. She quickly squelched the thought. Mac was leaving soon. Besides, with Jess to worry about and her new job starting soon, she had no time for anything else. Kissing Mac again or taking things further was out of the question.

She reached a four-way stop and braked. Hers was the only car. "For letting Mac in and out," she went on as she drove through the intersection, "Mr. and Mrs. Rutherford are waiving our rent next month."

Jesse angled his head at her. "That's good, right?"

Emmy had never hidden their money troubles from him. "You bet it is. Now I can decorate the rest of the house *before* I start at the library. I thought I'd pick up the paint tomorrow morning and get moving."

"More painting. Ugh!" Jess wrinkled his nose. "It's gonna stink."

"Only for a few days. And just think how much nicer the cottage will look." Enjoying this time with her son and reluctant to go home just yet, she made a spur-of-the-moment decision. "Why don't we stop for burgers tonight?"

She'd save the casserole for tomorrow.

Jesse licked his lips and rubbed his stomach. "Oh, boy."

Chapter Six

Monday morning, six long days since Mac had kissed Emmy, he turned the van onto Beach Cove Way like a thirsty horse headed for water. After taking Sunday off he was eager to see her, even if only for a few minutes in the morning and late afternoon.

He didn't want to feel this way. That he did put him in a foul mood. Thinking about Emmy all the time was driving him nuts. Jaw clamped, he slowed to a crawl.

He'd tried his damnedest to forget that he wanted her, had even taken out an old girlfriend, Dini Martin, Saturday night. As attractive as Dini was, Mac barely lasted through dinner, wishing he was with Emmy, instead. Kissing her again and more. The blood in his veins simmered and his groin stirred. Like a randy teenage boy, he spent his days and nights hot and bothered. Not fun. And he'd only kissed her the one time. If that wasn't a bad sign…

Swearing, he rounded the curve and her cottage came into view. The living-room drapes were open and lights inside glowed welcomingly. Mac didn't see Emmy, though. She started her new job today. Probably getting ready.

Jesse was already gone—moments earlier the bus had rattled by—which meant his mother was all by her lonesome.

Since Mac didn't expect Brian and Ian for another half hour, he, too, was alone. He imagined walking through her door, pulling her close and doing all the things he fantasized about. Palming her breasts, teasing her nipples, making her moan with need. She'd push close, wrap her thighs around his waist, and he'd…

A certain part of him rose to full attention, and he shifted uncomfortably. If his brothers ever found out about this… They wouldn't. It was only a matter of willpower and time. Once he left town, this fire torturing him would die. For now he'd best cool off.

The second he parked in front of the Rutherfords', Emmy's front door opened. She'd been watching for him, and he felt a surge of pleasure. Wearing a knee-length trench coat, heels and a pair of slacks, she hurried across the street.

Forgetting that he needed to get hold of himself, Mac exited the van with a thundering heart. "Hey," he said, meeting her at the porch steps.

"Hi." She sounded slightly winded, like she had the other day after those kisses.

Up close Mac noted her makeup and her hair, pulled back into a fancy twist. He liked what he saw. He also liked her without lipstick and her hair down. Man, he was in trouble.

"You look pretty for your first day at the library," he said as they started up the steps.

"Thanks." She patted her 'do as if checking to make sure it was okay. "I'm a little nervous."

"I'm sure you'll be fine. I saw the school bus leave."

"This morning it couldn't come soon enough." Crossing the porch beside him, she sighed. "Jess and I had another fight. He doesn't want the bus to drop him off at the library after school. He says it's uncool and that I should let him stay home alone. I'm not ready for that, and regardless what he thinks, he isn't, either."

"I hear you. Leaving kids on their own for hours after school is tempting trouble. When I was growing up, you wouldn't believe how much I hung out at the Halo Island Library. All those books to read and teach me new things? Ian and Brian spent a lot of afternoons there, too, while I worked. I remember a great after-school program they always talked about."

"Apparently that's been canceled," Emmy said. "One of my new responsibilities is to get a new program up and running and make certain it's successful. With all the kids sure to participate, I'm hoping Jesse makes a friend or two." She gave Mac a thoughtful look. "Maybe I'll ask your brothers how the program worked when they were in school and get their input. Do you think they'd mind?"

The way they felt about Emmy? Mac shook his head. "Not at all. I'll put in a good word about the library to Jesse. If I'd known, I'd have said something Saturday." The kid had stopped by and watched Mac work for a while, before Emmy had called him to lunch.

"Would you? That'd be wonderful." As she stood at the front door, her eyes shone. "Especially coming from you. He respects you so much, he might even listen."

An apt reminder that the boy needed a man's guidance. Mac wasn't that man and didn't want to be, but the thought of some other guy filling the role didn't sit well, either. Unwilling to consider what this might mean, he curled his hands into fists. "Bring him with you when you lock up tonight. I'll talk to him then."

"Okay, but I should warn you that I don't get off till six. If you don't want to wait around, that's okay. I'll bolt the door when I get home."

With his deadline? "I'm sure I'll still be here."

"Great, and thanks again." She pulled the key from her pocket.

With her eyes bright and warm and her mouth curled in gratitude, she was beautiful and beyond tempting. "Anything for you."

Hardly aware of his actions, he touched her face, trailing his fingers down the soft curve of her cheek. He traced her jawline and the smooth column of her neck. Felt her pulse bump. Breathed in her lemony scent. He'd never wanted a woman so much.

She swallowed and her glossy lips parted. It had been almost a week since he'd stood this close, smelled her and touched her skin—more than a red-blooded man in lust could take. His body went haywire.

"We shouldn't," she whispered, reading his mind.

The desire on her face only fanned his own need. "You're right, we shouldn't. But we're going to."

Her eyelids fluttered shut, the lashes dark against her pale skin. The key clattered against the wood porch floor, the sound ricocheting through the roar of desire in Mac's head.

What was he doing? Kissing Emmy again was way too risky, yet here he was, almost beyond caring. More rattled than he'd ever been in his life, he let her go and staggered back.

Her eyes popped open. They radiated confusion.

"As badly as I want to kiss you again, I won't do it," he said, his voice raspy with need.

Blinking, she touched her lips with her fingers. "I'm glad one of us can think straight," she agreed, the yearning expression belying her words.

And that was the problem. They both wanted more. A lot more.

Emmy pulled the lapels of her coat together. "It isn't smart to kiss each other. It's good that you stopped."

Good? Try hell. Mac retrieved the key. He thought about handing it to Emmy, but didn't. Touching her was too damned dangerous. He unlocked the house himself and left the key in the door.

Her fingers trembled as she removed it.

"Good luck with the library," he said, scraping his boots on the welcome mat.

"Thanks. Jess and I will see you late this afternoon."

He actually looked forward to her bringing the boy. The kid didn't know it, but he'd play the much-needed chaperone.

The Rutherfords were due home tomorrow. Couldn't be too soon.

FIFTEEN MINUTES after almost kissing Mac, Emmy pulled into the library's small, paved parking lot. Luckily traffic was light and she knew the way. She was too discombobulated to pay much attention to driving.

She'd just about convinced herself that she didn't want to kiss Mac again. Until he touched her face and gazed into her eyes with burning focus. Then she'd forgotten about everything except Mac and her desire. She couldn't ever remember wanting a man this way, and the feeling unnerved her.

Starting something with him was unwise, but in matters of the heart she never had been one for logic and reasoning. And around Mac she couldn't think straight to begin with. Though he was leaving soon, she wanted a relationship with him. There was no use worrying about Jesse getting attached. He already was.

So was Emmy. Thank goodness Mac had backed away. As she'd told him, one of them had to take control. It was a good thing her job started today. She was sure to be way too busy learning her way around the library and her new duties to think about Mac and this morning.

The library didn't open until ten, ninety minutes from now, but Sally Dorman, Emmy's new boss, had called an all-staff meeting to welcome her. There were three cars besides Emmy's in the lot, meaning she was the last to arrive. Light blazed cheerily through the windows of the one-story brick building. Her stomach in knots, purse and sack lunch in hand and ducking her head against the fine drizzle, Emmy dashed for the heavy, wood door. She knocked. Seconds later Sally gestured her inside.

"Hello, Emmy." The neat, compact, fiftysomething woman, who was about the age of Emmy's mother, smiled more warmly than Emmy ever remembered her mom smiling. "I'm glad you're here."

"Thanks. So am I." Emmy glanced around the pale blue walls. Libraries everywhere were much the same and she'd been interviewed here. The familiar bookshelves and stacks eased her shaky nerves.

"We're meeting in the staff room, behind the biography section. Follow me." Sally led the way past the fat beanbag chairs and stuffed animals grouped around the children's area. "All settled in?"

"Pretty much."

They passed through a doorway and into the staff room with its bulletin board, coatrack, refrigerator, microwave and coffeemaker. The other two employees were seated at the rectangular table in the middle of the room. "You remember Patty Fisher and Mason Jones from the interview," Sally said.

Patty, who Emmy guessed was in her early forties, and Mason, a round, balding man of about sixty, nodded and smiled. Both worked part-time, sharing the evening and Saturday shifts. Sally and now Emmy were the only full-time employees.

Returning the greetings, Emmy sat down at the table. She couldn't help noticing the bright pink box of doughnuts bearing the label Mocha Java. A cute little bakery café she'd driven past several times, but hadn't visited yet.

"I've worked here almost thirty years," Mason said. "That's ten years longer than Sally and fifteen more than Patty. I know I'm not alone in saying that we're happy to have you and your fresh energy in here."

"Amen." Patty smoothed her turtleneck pullover, a bright blue that set off her fair skin and dark hair.

They seemed as friendly as they had during the interview, and Emmy felt warm and welcome. She was going to like working here.

Sally nudged the doughnut box toward her. "These are heavenly. Help yourself. While we eat, we'll review the break and lunch schedules and discuss the after-school program."

As Emmy lifted the lid of the box, the scent of fresh-baked treats made her salivate. The chocolate doughnut she chose was still warm to the touch.

"Be warned, those things are addictive," Mason said.

"Since Sally started bringing them to our weekly staff meetings, I've had to let my belt out a notch."

"Haven't we all," Patty said, helping herself.

Sally winked at Emmy. "Any time you want me to stop buying them, just say the word."

"Deprive us? Never!" Mason looked appalled, and everyone chuckled. "You'll see, Emmy."

Emmy bit into the doughnut. Flavors exploded in her mouth, and she made a sound of pure enjoyment. Earning more laughs.

"Delicious," she proclaimed, already planning to take Jesse to the Mocha Java on Saturday morning. Maybe start a mother-son tradition.

After several minutes spent chatting, nibbling and reviewing the schedules, the talk turned to the after-school plans.

"We're thrilled that you'll be restarting the program," Patty said. "The last one ended five years ago when Jenny Standish retired. With so many latchkey kids on the island, we really need something."

"My son, Jesse, is one of them, so I have a vested interest," Emmy said. "He's in fifth grade and will be here this afternoon, so you'll get to meet him. I have a few ideas, but if any of you have suggestions, please share." She pulled a notebook and pen from her purse.

"You want to bring children in and keep them coming back," Sally said. "All kids love computers. That's a good place to start."

Mason brushed his mouth with a napkin. "I vote for regular storytellers who appeal to all age levels."

"Yes," Patty said. "And maybe offer various creative activities. Within limits, since this is a library and not an arts center."

All good suggestions Emmy jotted down. "I just learned that two men—they're twins—working on a renovation across the street from my house used to come to the after-school program. I thought I'd ask them what they'd liked."

"Great idea." Sally pushed the now-empty doughnut box aside. "You must be talking about Ian and Brian Struthers."

"How did you know?"

"I think they're the only male twins on the Island."

"From what I remember," Mason said, "they were good boys and big readers."

"They still are," Patty said. "Since they graduated college and moved back here, they've both come in when I've been working to check out books." She arched her eyebrows at Emmy. "If you've met Ian and Brian, you probably also know Mac. He's a big library user, too."

Emmy knew him, all right. Knew the feel of his arms around her and the warmth of his lips eagerly claiming hers. The aching desire to kiss him again— and more—flooded back. Flustered that she was thinking about Mac that way *now,* she managed a calm nod. "Yes, I've met him."

"After their parents died, Mac raised his brothers, you know," Sally said. "Such a tragic story, and such strong, brave kids."

Mason and Patty gave sympathetic nods.

Emmy wasn't surprised they knew about the Struthers family. On Halo Island, people cared about each other. The three librarians were looking at her, clearly waiting for a comment.

"Mac told me about that," she said.

"He did, did he?" Sally looked thoughtful. "That Mac Struthers brought up those boys and likes books is attractive in itself. And he's so good-looking."

"I know." Patty sighed. "I tell my husband he's lucky I'm in love with him or I'd be after Mac." She laughed. "Even if I *am* a good ten years older."

"Ladies, please." Mason rolled his eyes at Emmy. "If he knew what these two said about him, he'd never set foot in this library again."

"Then he'd better not find out." Sally shook a warning finger at him, her teasing smile taking away any sting. "What I find impossible to believe is that he's still available. In my opinion, any single woman who isn't interested in Mac Struthers is out of her mind."

The trio scrutinized Emmy as if checking on her sanity. They certainly were a nosy bunch.

"He can't get involved," she said, feeling an odd need to defend him. "He's leaving soon to travel and then go to school."

"That's just an excuse." Sally waved her arm in a dismissive gesture. "I went to college years after I got married, and still managed to work part-time and raise my two boys while I earned my degree. Mac could do the same. And another thing. Who says he needs to travel alone? But he's a smart one. Once he finds the right woman, he'll figure all that out."

Though no one glanced at Emmy, she felt as if the words were meant for her. Face burning, she bent over her notebook, pretending to jot something down.

As EMMY SHRUGGED into her coat, said her goodbyes and left the library with Jesse at the end of her first day, she felt good, but also tired and hungry. And cranky. So was her son. Regardless, she was determined to enjoy the short drive home.

While pulling out of the parking lot, she struck up a conversation. "I love this library, and the other librarians seem nice, don't you think?"

"I guess, but there aren't many kids around. If I stayed home by myself, I'd have more fun."

Refusing to get sucked into the same old argument, she ignored the comment and forced a cheerful note. "At least you finished your homework."

"I had to. With other people hogging the computers there was nothing else to do."

"You could always check out a book or a magazine. You know, read."

"Yeah, I know, Mom. But books aren't the same as friends."

"They can be. When I was a little girl—"

"Books kept you from feeling lonely," he finished, rolling his eyes. "You only told me that a billion times."

Patience thinning, Emmy hurried on. "Anyway, once the after-school program starts, I guarantee there'll be loads of kids here. Probably some from your class."

"I don't like any of them," Jesse grumbled. "And they don't like me."

Emmy's heart ached for him. "They just don't know you yet."

After a full week of school, her son had yet to make a single friend. At least he was dressing decently. Instead of gang T-shirts and too-baggy jeans, he now wore T-shirts with movie or cartoon drawings, and jeans or cargo pants that actually fit. All he needed was an extra push. The after-school program would help, Emmy hoped.

"Brian and Ian used to come to the library after-school program," she said.

"They did?"

She nodded. "I'm going to talk to them about it, right after I pop tonight's dinner into the oven." Over the weekend she'd made and frozen a pot of stew and enough casseroles to last the entire workweek, which gave her more evening time to spend with Jesse.

"Mac really likes the library, too." Her headlights hit the Beach Cove Way sign, and she slowed and signaled. "Wow, we're almost home. Already." The short, easy drive was worlds different from the nearly one-hour traffic-congested commute in Oakland.

As Emmy rounded the curve, the lone streetlight at the far end of the cul-de-sac silhouetted her own dark house and the bright lights of the Rutherfords'. Ian and Brian were ambling toward their truck, obviously finished for the day. If she hoped to talk with them before they left, warming up dinner would have to wait.

The instant she braked to a stop in the driveway, Jesse's seat belt slid apart. He opened the door.

"Wait," she said, but he was already loping across the street.

Emmy followed with fresh worries. Jesse was getting far too attached to Mac and his brothers, and there wasn't a thing she could do about it.

Her son knocked, then disappeared through the front door, where judging by the light, Mac was still working. Knowing she'd see him in a few moments filled Emmy with giddy anticipation, but because she only expected a hello and goodbye and she needed to talk with Ian and Brian, she turned away from the light and hurried toward the truck.

"Don't leave just yet," she called out.

"Hey, Emmy." Ian, who was texting on his phone, closed it and grinned. "What's up?"

"How was your first day at the library?" Brian asked.

"Great, thanks. Listen, I'm putting together a new after-school program and since you're veterans of the old one, I'd like to pick your brains."

"Anytime," Ian said.

Brian nodded. "Just say when."

"How about tomorrow night? Come for dinner at six-thirty." She'd defrost all the stew—thank goodness she'd frozen enough for several meals—and during lunch break tomorrow, pick up bread and salad fixings.

Brian rubbed his hands together. "You're on."

"What should we bring?" Ian asked.

"Just yourselves and a willingness to talk."

The men said their good-nights and slid into their seats. Seconds later the truck pulled onto the street.

As Emmy moved toward the steps of the Rutherfords' house, her cell phone rang. The LED identified the caller as Tom Rutherford. He and Melinda were due back tomorrow.

"I'm about to lock up your house," Emmy said after they exchanged greetings. "I'll bet you can't wait to see what's going on in your kitchen."

"Mac forwarded some photos, which helps." Tom cleared his throat. "I'm afraid we're going to have to postpone seeing the real thing. How do you feel about taking care of the house a while longer? Melinda's uncle needs us to stay, and we figure we'll be here at least another two weeks."

Two more weeks of facing Mac twice a day. Filled

with misgivings, Emmy climbed the steps. "If you'd rather, I could give Mac the key," she said.

"Melinda prefers that you hold on to it. Is that a problem?"

Only for her heart, which seemed to care more every time she saw the man. "None at all," Emmy said.

"You're a lifesaver. Everything okay with the cottage?"

"Just fine. I painted the whole interior. I think you and Melinda will like the change." The cottage was so much brighter and cheerier now.

"I'm sure we will. We'll be in touch." Tom disconnected.

Mac needed to know about the Rutherfords. Emmy knocked, and when no one answered, opened the door. For some reason hesitant to go inside, she stood on the threshold. The smell of new wood filled her nostrils. Bright light from the bare bulb hanging from the kitchen ceiling cast deep shadows across the kitchenwares piled everywhere.

"Jesse," she called out. "Time to go home now and warm up dinner."

"Hear that?" she heard Mac say. "Dinner." He sounded envious. "You'd best go."

Due to the cramped space the two males entered the living room in single file, Jesse first, then Mac. Emmy drank in the sight of him. The man sure knew how to fill out jeans and a flannel workshirt. Oh, she had it bad. By the adoring look on Jesse's face, he did, too.

Whatever would they do when he left town?

"Tom Rutherford just called," she told Mac. "Melinda's uncle is still sick, so they won't be back for another two weeks."

"Bummer."

Mac looked at her and she knew he was thinking the same thing. That they were better off not seeing each other. There was a solution. She could unlock the door before he arrived and bolt it after he left, but Emmy knew she wouldn't do that. She'd wait for Mac every morning and assume he'd hang around for her after work.

"Jesse and I were talking about the library," Mac said, clapping her son's shoulder. "One of my favorite places to hang out."

While Jesse looked at the floor, Emmy mouthed a silent thank-you.

Mac nodded. "Did you get a chance to talk to Ian and Brian about their after-school program?"

"Not yet, but they're coming to dinner tomorrow night to answer questions." Emmy couldn't leave Mac out, nor did she want to. "You're welcome, too."

"Better not." His eyes flashed regret.

Jesse looked crestfallen. "Don't you like us?"

"Sure I do, but I don't want to get in the way or stifle the conversation. There's no reason for me to come."

His gaze stayed on her son, but Emmy knew he was speaking to her. Given their strong mutual attraction, staying away did seem best. Yet she wanted him at her dinner table. Just this once.

"You don't need a reason," Jesse said. "My mom's a good cook. You'll like her food. You *have* to eat with us. Right, Mom?"

Jesse gave her the big-eyed, pleading look she couldn't resist. With her son and Mac's brothers around she and Mac ought to be safe enough from temptation. "Please come," Emmy said.

He hesitated, then shrugged. "Okay, I'll be there. But I can't stay long. I'll leave right after dinner."

Chapter Seven

"That was a great meal," Ian said as he wiped his mouth on his napkin.

Brian patted his slightly rounded belly. "Much better than what we usually have."

Mac nodded. "You weren't kidding about your mom's cooking, Jesse." He glanced at Emmy. "Thanks."

Crowded around the small square table built for four normal-size people, Jesse and the three brawny brothers had demolished the stew, two large loaves of garlic bread, a huge bowl of salad and the three-dozen chocolate-chip cookies that were supposed to last all week. Emmy didn't mind. Having guests was fun. Especially the Struthers men, who kept up a lively, enjoyable conversation, in which Jess enthusiastically participated.

"You're welcome." Contented from the warm and friendly masculine attention she rarely got, and imagining that this was what a happy family felt like, Emmy smiled.

As she reached for the water pitcher to top up empty glasses, her elbow bumped Mac.

"Excuse me." She jerked back, but not before awareness spread through her. Though she didn't so much as glance at him, she sensed his sudden tension.

"That's okay," he said, wiping his mouth.

Thanks to the lack of space, this wasn't the first time that some part of their bodies—thighs, arms, feet—had connected. Despite the layers of clothing they both wore, with every contact Emmy's nerves hummed and thrilled with anticipation. Thank goodness no one at the table read minds, or she'd be totally embarrassed.

Mac accepted a refill, then pushed his chair back, creating much-needed room. He drained the glass like a man on fire.

Emmy began to stack plates, but Ian stopped her.

"You cooked. We'll clean up. Relax and take it easy."

With Mac sitting beside her? Ha! She shook her head. "You're guests here. Besides, you already helped me so much. I really appreciate the input from the three of you about the after-school program. Your input, too, Jesse," she added.

Input her son might never have given without the Struthers men's encouragement. He actually seemed excited about the library, and Emmy was more than grateful. "Thanks to you all, the new program will be wonderful."

"Once you get the thing up and running, let Ian and me know and we'll stop in," Brian said.

A terrific idea popped into her mind. "What if I have you come in and talk about construction?" The twins were so cute and personable and entertaining that boys and girls alike would enjoy listening to them.

"Uh, okay, sure," Ian said. "We'll bring tools the kids can try out."

Jess grinned. "Cool."

Brian glanced at Mac. "You're a lot more experienced than we are. If Emmy schedules us while you're still in town, you should join us."

Mac's younger brothers shared a quick glance, and Emmy wondered what he'd do if he knew they didn't want to run his company.

"I can't spare the time," he said. "Right now, neither can you two. That talk will have to wait till we've done more at the Rutherfords'."

"Sure," Brian said.

"Come on, Jesse." Ian beckoned the boy to stand. "The three of us will make short work of this dinner mess."

Looking torn, as if he couldn't decide whether or not to join them, Jesse fidgeted in his seat. "I want to, but I have math homework. I couldn't do it at the library because I don't get it, and my mom doesn't, either."

"Math never has been a strength of mine," Emmy admitted.

"It's due tomorrow, and Mrs. Hatcher expects me to hand in all my work on time. Maybe I should study instead?"

Mac sat back, watching through slightly narrowed eyes, and Emmy knew he wondered what she'd do. Jesse was supposed to clear the table and load the dishwasher after dinner, but rarely did. Now was a good time to show both Mac and Jesse that she could be firm.

"You'll have time for your math after you help Ian and Brian," she said decisively. Mac's approving nod pleased her.

Jesse looked this side of stunned and not quite ready to accept that she meant business. "But this stuff is really hard," he grumbled. "It'll take me hours to figure it out."

"You still have to do your chores," Mac said. "Like

Ian said, with the three of you working together, cleanup won't take long."

"If I have to," Jess grumbled. He glared at Emmy. "But if I get in trouble for not finishing the problems, it's your fault."

Emmy wavered, but before she could speak, Brian did.

"Here's an idea," he said as he stacked plates. "Let Mac help with your homework. He always gave us a hand. He's a math whiz."

Eagerness lit Jesse's face. "You are?"

Mac looked wary, as if he realized that Jesse was getting too close and didn't know what to do about it.

"Mac can't stay late. Remember?" Emmy was giving the man a valid out. "He's been working all day, and I'm sure he's tired and ready to go home."

Jesse glanced at the silverware he was collecting and gave a listless nod that hurt to see. "That's okay, Mac." Clutching the cutlery in his fists, he turned toward the sink.

No one said a word. Did Ian and Brian think Mac should stay? What was Mac thinking? With all their faces carefully blank, Emmy had no clue. Fighting the need to fold Jesse in a comforting hug, she laced her fingers together in her lap.

Someone turned on the faucet. Water swished through the silence.

Lips compressed, Mac glanced at the ceiling. He blew out a breath. "Okay, Jesse," he said over the running tap. "You clean up, then I'll get you started. I'll stay another half hour, but after that, I'm gone."

SITTING AT the kitchen table while Jesse labored over a long-division problem, Mac munched a fresh-baked cookie and skimmed through the weekly Halo Island

News Emmy had handed him. The newly painted kitchen, now a warm peach color, felt cheerful and homey. Especially with her in it. Wearing a checkered, food-spattered bib apron, she stood at the counter with her back to him and Jesse, mixing up cookie batter. Since Mac and his brothers had cleaned her out of chocolate chips, these were oatmeal raisin. The house smelled better than a bakery at dawn. How she found the energy after working all day, then serving a great meal, mystified him.

Even more amazing was her silence. After Ian and Brian had left, she explained that she didn't want to interrupt her son's homework time with conversation. Which was a good idea, but most women would've jabbered away regardless. Not Emmy. The quiet was working well for Jesse, too. Deep in concentration, the boy seemed unaware of his mother's presence.

Whereas Mac was tuned in to her every move. The way she brushed the hair out of her eyes with her upper arm. How she dried her hands on the apron after washing them. That she cleaned up her mess as she went along, occasionally snitching raw dough and making soft sounds of pleasure when she popped it into her mouth.

At the moment she was carefully placing rounded spoonfuls of dough on a cookie sheet. The apron tie at her back was working loose, the ribbons trailing down her sweet behind. Mac pictured her in nothing but the apron. He imagined knotting those ties for her, then cupping her round cheeks. Better yet, pulling the bow apart and tugging that apron off…

His body tightened. What else was new? Fantasizing this much and this often was seriously killing him. He needed to forget Emmy, to leave right now. He glanced at the clock. Hell, he'd been here forty-five minutes, fifteen minutes longer than he'd planned.

Jesse muttered and scrubbed a worn eraser over his paper. He glanced at Mac with a confused look, and Mac knew he'd stay as long as the kid needed him.

When he should be running for his life.

"Need help?" he asked.

The boy nodded. "This answer looks wrong, but I can't figure out why."

Mac looked over the problem. As he explained what to do, the timer buzzed. Unable to stop himself, he watched Emmy slip her hands into oven mitts and pull a sheet of baked cookies from the oven. Which gave him yet another great view of her rear. He turned back to Jesse to find the kid studying him with a curious expression. The boy glanced at his mother, then at Mac again. A sly grin bloomed on his face.

As if he thought there was something between Mac and his mom. There was, but it wasn't going anyplace. Mac changed his mind about sticking around.

"You can take it from here on your own," he said, pushing his chair back.

In the process of moving the cookies onto the cooling rack, Emmy glanced up. Her face was flushed from the oven heat, and once again her hair swung loose from behind her ear. "It's almost Jesse's bedtime, anyway." She looked at her son. "Are you about through?"

"Just about." Still bent over the paper, Jesse continued to work. Moments later he laid down his pencil. "Now I'm done."

"You picked that up fast," Mac said, giving the boy a nod of approval. "You're a smart kid with a good head for math."

Looking as if he'd won a trophy, Jesse beamed. Emmy smiled, too, a pure, happy expression that went straight into Mac's chest. A ray of warmth that coaxed out his own grin.

For one long moment Mac held her gaze, then she jerked her attention to Jesse, who by his knowing look hadn't missed a thing.

"Time for your shower," Emmy said.

"And time for me to go," Mac said. "Thanks again for feeding me tonight." He stood and brought the empty cookie plate to Emmy. "And for the cookies."

"Dinner was the least I could do. What do you say to Mac, Jesse?"

"Thanks for helping me with my math." The boy jumped up. "You don't have to leave yet, Mac. My mom goes to bed pretty late."

Bed and Emmy. A dangerous combination. For his own good, Mac definitely needed out of here. "But I don't," he said. "In fact, I'm about ready to turn in."

"But it's only eight-forty-five." Jesse looked incredulous.

"Hey, I'm up at five every morning, and I work hard all day. I like a good night's sleep."

Unless he happened to share his bed with a willing woman. Which he hadn't in months. Too busy and too focused on enrolling in school and his trip. Even so he was primed and more than ready for a night of passion with Emmy. He quickly nixed the thought. Not with this woman, not in this house.

Jesse disappeared. Emmy slipped out of her apron. "I'm so grateful for what you did for Jesse tonight," she said as she walked Mac to the door. "Your brothers were right—you're great with kids."

Suddenly hip-hop music blared, filling the house. The shower started.

"He turns it up so he can hear over the water," Emmy said, shaking her head.

"Like I said, I didn't mind helping him. But, Emmy, I think he's getting too attached."

"You noticed that, too." Worry wrinkled the space between her eyebrows. "I'm not sure what to do." Hand on the doorknob, she paused. "Do you have any ideas?"

"I'll do my best to steer clear of him." Though so far that hadn't worked.

"And I'll try to keep him away from you and your brothers. Now that he's coming to the library every afternoon, he won't see much of you. That'll help. I hope."

Mac hated the concern darkening her face. "I'll also talk to him and make sure he understands that I won't be sticking around."

"Thanks. You really are wonderful." Emmy opened the front door.

Any fool could see that she was as bad off as her son, liking Mac more than she should. This was not good. Mac counted himself lucky that he didn't share those same feelings for her.

Right, and the outside temperature was ninety degrees.

As the damp, cold sea air rushed in, he brushed her hair back. "Thanks again for this evening."

Intending a quick good-night, he brushed his lips lightly over hers. But she leaned in and looped her arms around his neck. And he was exactly where he'd wanted to be since the last time he'd kissed her. Holding her close.

This was wrong. And dangerous. But Mac could no longer fight himself. With a groan, he gave in.

HERE SHE WAS, kissing Mac again. Emmy sighed. *At last.* She shouldn't, but his arms felt so good around her. His tongue teased hers, darting in and out. He tasted of oatmeal cookie and man and need, and she eagerly returned his kisses.

Warm hands clasped her hips, anchoring her tightly against his hard body. He was aroused, proof that he wanted her as badly as she wanted him. That they were both lost. She wriggled closer.

An approving sound rumbled from Mac's chest, and his avid kisses turned scorching. Emmy's muscles loosened. Her bones softened and seemed to melt. If not for Mac holding her up, she'd surely have sunk to the floor.

Sometime later—or mere seconds, she had no idea— he slid his palms up her sides. It had been so long. Craving his hands on her breasts, attuned to his every move, Emmy leaned back a fraction, silently begging him. Finally he cupped her breasts.

Pleasure pulsed through her. Nipples stiffening, she moaned into his mouth. She let go of his shoulders to guide his hands under her sweater. He palmed her through her bra, then slipped his fingers inside the cups, teasing her sensitive tips.

Dear God. Desire flared in every inch of her body. Arching back, she thrust her breasts more deeply into his hands. "My bra unhooks in the back," she urged.

An instant later she felt it loosen and open. Mac pushed the cotton up, scraping her swollen nipples.

"I want you," he gasped, his breath hot against her ear.

"Mmm, me, too."

His soft lips nibbled her neck while his fingers gently plucked her nipples. It felt so good. Moisture pooled between her legs. Fevered and craving contact *right there,* she hooked her leg around Mac's thigh, bringing the most aching part of her flush against his rigid arousal. Even though they were both fully dressed, she was so stimulated she was on the verge of climaxing. If Mac didn't make love with her right now…

"Please," she whispered.

Growling, he ground his hips. "Don't tempt me."

Somehow through her haze of need she heard the shower shut off. Mac must've noticed it, too, for they pulled away from each other at the same time.

Reaching behind her, he deftly fastened her bra like a man with plenty of experience. Then he tugged her sweater over her hips.

"Good night, Emmy." He touched her cheek briefly, turned away and moved purposefully toward his van.

In a daze she leaned against the doorjamb. Only after he glanced at her before sliding into the driver's seat did she realize she was standing in the open doorway. With the furnace on full blast, heating the great outdoors. An expense she certainly didn't need.

Not that she was cold after what had just happened. Her pulse chaotic, she closed the door, leaned dreamily against it and hugged herself.

Abruptly the hip-hop music stopped. Seconds later, as Jesse padded noisily toward the living room, Emmy hastily checked her hair.

Wearing flannel pajama bottoms and a Bone Thugs-n-Harmony T-shirt, Emmy's son stopped in the hallway. "Is Mac gone?"

Not trusting herself to speak just yet, she nodded.

"Mom? Are you okay? Your cheeks are red and your lips look funny."

"I ate a cookie that was too hot and burned myself," she shamelessly lied.

About the cookie, not the burned lips. Mac's passionate kisses had seared her mouth.

"Tonight was really cool. Can we invite Mac and his brothers over for dinner again?"

This was a good time to discuss the fact that Mac wasn't going to be around much longer. But Emmy was still dazed and not thinking clearly. She decided to save that conversation for another day. "We'll see," she said. "Now, off you go to bed."

Later, while she filled the cookie jar, she thought about what had happened at the door. About Mac's kisses, his hands on her breasts. And about her own inflamed response. Brazenly hooking her leg around his thigh, practically begging him to make love to her.

As she remembered now, her cheeks warmed. But at the time she hadn't been the least self-conscious or embarrassed. She'd wanted him that badly.

So badly she'd forgotten to close the door, had almost forgotten that her own son was in the house. Unbelievable!

If that wasn't bad enough, she was close to being in love with Mac Struthers. Any fool knew that meant pain and a broken heart. Emmy didn't want that, nor could she afford the distraction. Not when Jesse needed her. More than ever once Mac left.

"I have to stop," she told herself. Stop caring and stop this reckless yearning.

Yet despite the warning and all the valid reasons, despite the risks, she wanted more with Mac. After years of celibacy her body was awake and alive, starved for his touch.

At eleven she checked on Jesse, then crawled into bed, exhausted. But as she tossed and turned and burned for Mac, she wondered whether she'd ever fall asleep.

Chapter Eight

When Mac pulled into the dirt lot of the building-supply store on the edge of town, the early-morning rush was in full swing. Trucks and vehicles of all kinds crowded the area. What a pain. Grumbling, he slowly circled the yard, searching for a place to park.

He didn't need the oak flooring until late this afternoon and could've waited to pick it up or sent one of his brothers. But that meant stopping work in the middle of things, which he didn't want to do. Besides, if he stayed here long enough his brothers would beat him to the Rutherfords'. Let *them* deal with Emmy this morning. After almost losing control last night, Mac wasn't ready to face her.

"Coward," he muttered.

Beeping in warning, a flatbed truck on the far side of the lot began to back out, and Mac drove over to park. Signaling, he let the van idle and waited. He and Emmy should talk, but not just yet, not with him wanting her as he did. Not until he pulled it together and reined in his lust.

Good thing Ian and Brian were clueless about this physical thing between him and Emmy. They liked her and if they had any idea what had happened last night, they'd be on his case for sure. Pressuring him about what he should and shouldn't do. They didn't want her hurt.

Mac didn't, either, and as fiercely as he wanted to make love with her—he thought of little else—he didn't intend to do anything about it. No more kisses. Nothing else. Not even if she looped her arms around his neck, begging with her eyes and mouth.

At last the flatbed *putt-putted* away. Still thinking about Emmy, Mac pulled into the slot. All that passion simmering inside her, her eager response to his kisses tempting him to bring it to a boil…

His jeans grew annoyingly tight. Calling himself a fool, he shifted unhappily in his seat. Best not get out of the van just yet. His hormones were raging like a fifteen-year-old kid's, and he was sick and tired of it. He needed sex and soon. One night of passion. But Emmy was a forever-type woman. Even if Mac hadn't been leaving in a month and nothing would stop him, he couldn't handle a serious relationship.

Jim Applebaum, a high-school buddy of Ian and Brian, was throwing a party Friday night and Mac was invited. He'd turned Jim down, but now… Ian and Brian claimed that more than a few available women would be there. The idea of hooking up with someone who wanted what he did—one night of no-strings sex—appealed to Mac. That ought to take his mind off Emmy. He shoved aside the memory that a similar plan involving Dini Martin had failed. Mac was at breaking point. If he didn't take a woman home tomorrow night, he might just lose his mind.

When his body settled down enough that he wouldn't embarrass himself, he exited the van and walked past the chain-link fence where lumber was stacked. He entered the vast, squat building, which looked just like any other home-improvement superstore, nodding at clerks he recognized.

Mac headed for Receiving and took his place in the line of builders and do-it-yourselfers, behind a short, wiry man he knew. Gus Jenkins was several decades older and had given Mac his first construction job. Once Mac had started his own business, Gus had mentored him like the father Mac had always wanted. But these days they didn't see much of each other.

Grinning, Mac clapped his friend on the shoulder. "Hey, Gus. How goes it?"

"As I live and breathe." Gus's face lit up. "You're looking good. I hear you're finally cutting loose to travel like you always wanted."

Mac nodded. "When I get back, I'll start college and finally earn my degree."

"Can't go wrong doing that. You worked so hard building your company. You're not going to let it die, are you?"

"No way. Ian and Brian will run it for me."

"Ian and Brian?"

Gus knew they'd worked for Mac on and off, so the astonished look that crossed his face puzzled Mac. Before he could question his old friend, the clerk beckoned Gus forward.

"About time," Gus muttered. "If I don't see you before you leave, have a great time. And send me a postcard."

Fifteen minutes later, Mac gaped at the clerk across the counter. "What do you mean, my flooring isn't ready?"

"Shipping mix-up. Sorry, Mac. We just found out ourselves. We were gonna call you."

Instead, here he was, wasting time when he could've been working. "When *will* it get here?" he asked.

The clerk pointed to his computer screen. "Looks like Monday afternoon."

Which meant waiting until Tuesday to lay the floor—five days from now. Mac frowned. "I can't afford to wait that long." Not with his tight schedule.

"You don't have much choice. 'Less you want drive over to Seattle and pick it up yourself."

Mac considered doing just that. Even though it meant a forty-five-minute ferry ride to Anacortes followed by a ninety-minute drive to Seattle, plus more time to navigate city traffic. Then another hour or so to load the boards into the van. Add in the return trip and the day was shot. Still better than waiting five days.

He'd send one of his brothers. No, both. They'd probably welcome a trip off the island. And by getting rid of them he wouldn't have to hear them yammer about Emmy and pretend he didn't care.

He checked his watch. By now they'd be at the Rutherfords' and Emmy would have left for work. Perfect.

On his way to the van Mac called Brian's cell to tell him about the flooring and to let him know he'd changed his mind about Jim Applebaum's party tomorrow night.

Feeling much better now, he whistled as he drove toward the Rutherfords'.

THROUGHOUT THE mostly quiet day, Emmy helped library patrons find and check out books, chatted with Sally and firmed up plans for the after-school program. She also thought about Mac, whom she hadn't seen this morning. Instead, for the first time, Ian and Brian had arrived first.

She'd greeted them with a smile and had unlocked the door, all the while pretending she didn't care whether or not she saw their brother today. For, she *did* care, and her disappointment was as sharp as a kitchen knife.

Thankfully oblivious, Brian and Ian had again thanked her for dinner and hinted that they'd like to come again. Emmy hadn't known what to say. She wasn't about to explain that what had begun as a friendly meal had ended with her and Mac kissing and more. Or that she'd spent a restless night replaying what had happened, kicking herself for getting so carried away, yet at the same time not at all sorry. So she'd simply ignored their suggestion of sharing another meal.

Tired as she was, her nerves hummed and her body ached for more with Mac. Too bad, since she wasn't about to let anything else happen.

Pushing the man from her thoughts, she yawned. "It sure is slow today," she told Mason, who'd just started his afternoon shift and was helping her sort through returned books.

"Thursdays usually are—don't ask me why," he said. "Just a quirk of our little library. Where's our illustrious boss this afternoon?"

"She left early for a doctor's appointment."

"Good day for it. How're you doing with your after-school plans?"

A question Emmy jumped on with enthusiasm. "I'm really excited about the program and hope to start next week," she finished after giving Mason the details. "Say, would you mind reading over the flyer I designed? Sally and Patty already did, but I'd like your input, too." She planned to post the flyer at the grocery store, at Halo Island School and here at the library.

"Happy to. Leave it on my desk and I'll take a look after I shelve these books."

"Would you like help?"

Mason shook his head. "Why don't you stay at the front desk in case someone needs you?"

With business so slow, Emmy doubted anyone would. She glanced at the clock, thankful that it was almost three-thirty. Any minute, Jesse would walk in. Today she might even be able to help him with his homework.

When the front door opened, Emmy leaned on the waist-high counter anticipating Jesse. She wanted to run to meet him, but that would only embarrass him. But instead of Jess, a small, thin boy wandered in. He wore a parka and carried a backpack much like her son's, his blond hair windblown and his eyes round and solemn. Looking as if he'd never been inside Halo Island Library and was intimidated, he glanced furtively about him.

Poor little guy. When he finally noticed Emmy, she offered a welcoming smile. The boy made a beeline for her.

"Hello," she said softly, so as not to disturb the handful of people in the building. "I'm Ms. Logan, the new librarian. Actually, I'm new to Halo Island."

"Me, too." That explained the lost look. Emmy put a finger to her lips and the boy lowered his voice.

"We just moved here Monday. My name is Peter Wysocki."

"Nice to meet you, Peter. I can't believe you're new in town, too. What a coincidence. Jesse, my son, and I arrived about two weeks ago. We're from Oakland."

"Is that anywhere near Green Valley?"

A place Emmy had never heard of. "I'm not sure. Is that in Washington?"

Peter nodded.

"Oakland is in California."

"Oh. My dad got laid off from the lumber mill. So we moved here. We're opening a gift shop on Main Street."

The street, which ran through Halo Island's downtown area, was half a mile from the library. "Ah. That's a great location for a business."

"My mom says lots of tourists shop there in the summer."

"That's what I hear."

Peter was talkative and open, exactly the sort of friend Emmy envisioned for her son. She wondered if they were the same age. This boy was smaller, but seemed about as mature as Jesse.

"Jesse's eleven," Emmy said. "How old are you?"

"I turned eleven right before Christmas." Peter slid off his backpack and set it beside him. Then he slipped out of his coat, letting it fall to the floor.

"Another coincidence. Are you in Mrs. Hatcher's class, too?"

He shook his head, making his fine, blond hair bounce. "I'm in fourth grade. I have Miss Madison." He glanced again around the library. "Where's Jesse now?"

"I expect him soon. Did you ride the school bus here?"

"Yeah."

Then where was Jesse? Emmy's stomach tightened. Her son knew he was supposed to get off the bus at the end of the block and come straight to the library. Which he still wasn't happy about. This morning they'd argued yet again about it. He might be taking his time, just to get her goat.

She'd give him five minutes. If he didn't walk through the door by then, she'd march outside and find him.

Peter's shoulders hunched and he seemed to shrink into himself, and Emmy imagined she looked pretty worried. She smoothed her expression. "Are you looking for a particular book?"

He shook his head. "My parents are working. I'm to wait here till they pick me up. I'm supposed to do my homework. Is it okay if I use the computer?"

Obviously Peter was a latchkey child, whose mother and father preferred that he sit in the library rather than stay home alone. Emmy approved. This child was the perfect candidate for the after-school program.

"We have two, and they're right over there," she said, pointing. "We usually limit your time to thirty minutes so that everyone gets a turn. But since at the moment no one else seems interested, feel free to use it as long as you like."

As Peter turned toward the computers she stopped him. "I'm starting a special program for kids ages six to fifteen," she said. "Monday through Friday, from three-thirty till six. You'll have time for homework, but we'll also learn about and try fun things. Interesting speakers, arts and crafts, storytellers, things like that. I haven't finished the information flyer yet, but I'll have it tomorrow. You can take one home and share it with your parents. Or I could talk with them when they pick you up."

"Sure."

The door opened again and Jesse trudged through. Emmy let out a breath of relief. "Here's Jesse now."

Her son had tied his jacket around his waist. His cheeks were red from the cold, and Emmy bet goose-flesh covered his bare arms. He should've worn his coat, but she wasn't about to fight with him about that now.

She waved, but Jesse pretended not to see. Afraid he'd turn up his nose if she introduced him to Peter, she stayed back and let the boys meet on their own.

She watched them circle each other and eavesdropped when they finally spoke.

"I saw you on the bus," Jesse said.

"I'm Peter Wysocki. That's Polish."

"I'm Jesse. Hey."

"Hey. Your mom said you're in fifth grade."

"You talked with my mom?" Jesse shot a horrified look Emmy's way, and she was glad she hadn't butted in.

"She's nice," Peter said. "I'll have Mrs. Hatcher next year. I hear she's pretty cool."

After shooting Emmy a guarded look—why, she didn't know—Jesse ground the toe of his sneaker into the blue carpet. "She's okay, I guess."

The boys looked as if they might continue chatting. Not wanting to interfere, Emmy pointed to a nearby table and left them to it. Peter never did use the computer.

His mother picked him up just before six, at the end of Emmy's shift. The friendly, but harried woman only spared Emmy a few minutes to discuss the after-school program, but by the time she and Peter left, Emmy had her first enrollee, aside from Jesse. And Jess had made his first friend on the island.

Not bad for a slow Thursday.

As EMMY DROVE through town, Jess began to squirm in his seat. "Do you think Mac and his brothers are still working?"

"I suspect Ian and Brian have finished for the day," Emmy said. "But Mac is probably there."

Her heart lifted at the thought before uncertainty churned through her. Facing Mac after last night… Was he sorry he'd kissed her? Would she feel uncomfortable and tense? What would he say? What would *she* say?

Silly worrying that reminded her of her high-school days. She and Mac were adults who'd kissed. That wasn't any big deal. Even so, she was glad of Jess's company.

"Can we invite him to dinner?"

Emmy shook her head. "I don't think we should."

"Why not?"

Because with Mac in the house she couldn't think straight. "He ate with us last night," she said. "I doubt he'll want to do it again so soon."

The rest of the way home, Jess stayed quiet, and Emmy assumed the matter was closed. Adult or not, anxieties about seeing Mac ate at her. She needed a plan. The only one she could think of was to stay calm and rational and at least five feet away from him at all times. That would certainly help.

As she'd predicted, Mac's van was still parked in front of the Rutherfords'. The second she rolled to a stop in the driveway, Jess bolted from the car.

"What's the hurry?" she asked.

"I'm going across the road to invite Mac for dinner."

WITHOUT HIS BROTHERS around Mac had spent a productive, quiet day mudding drywall, measuring and cutting molding for the floor, and tying up several loose ends on the remodeling project. To his relief he'd also managed to keep his mind off Emmy. He'd barely thought of her or her son all day. At last he was in control of himself again, which felt damned good. He was even charged about that party tomorrow night.

And bone tired from a day of hard work. But he couldn't quit just yet. He wanted the walls ready for a final sanding before he and his brothers laid the floor. That meant re-mudding them tonight, which would take several more hours.

He was stretching his back and wondering whether the energy bar in his shirt pocket would hold him until he finished when two sets of footsteps thudded across the porch.

Mac knew they belonged to Jesse and Emmy. His spirits brightened. He wiped his hands on his jeans and headed for the door. And then frowned. Not because he cared about them, he told himself, just looked forward to company after a long day alone.

Yeah, right.

He opened the door and Jesse rushed inside, breathless. Emmy stayed on the step, hovering in the shadows cast by the yellow porch light. As if she was afraid to get too close. She opened her mouth to speak, but Jesse never gave her the chance.

"Hi, Mac. Want to come for dinner tonight?"

"Uh…" Mac glanced at Emmy. Big mistake. Her luminous gaze hooked him, and the physical hunger he was sure he'd banished gnawed at him once again.

Her eyebrows lifted and he realized she expected him to warn Jesse about getting too attached. For a moment he forgot the boy's question. Oh, yeah, dinner.

Mac cleared his throat and pinned his attention on her kid. "I'm leaving in a month and I'm not coming back for about three years." Except maybe over the holidays. "You know that, right?"

"So?" the boy said. "You still have to eat dinner. Come to our house tonight."

Nuts as it was, Mac considered doing just that. And promptly shelved the idea. For his sake and Emmy's, he'd stay away. He shook his head. "Thanks, but there's a lot left to do around here this evening, and I'd like to get home before midnight."

"Oh." Jesse dipped his head, then caught his lower lip between his teeth. "How about tomorrow?"

"Jesse! Mac probably has plans on Friday night."

Despite the dim light, Mac noted the pink flooding Emmy's face. He nodded. "I do."

"See? I'll bet he has a date."

Shadows hid her expression, but Mac sensed her curiosity. He shook his head and thought he saw her shoulders relax. "I'm going to a party with Ian and Brian."

"How fun."

Her voice sounded artificially bright. Go figure. "Yeah, it should be a blast," Mac said.

Emmy beckoned to Jesse. "We should go now. Mac, please let me know when you're ready to lock up."

A good hour later, as Mac spread mud over the drywall seams, his mind once again filled with thoughts of Emmy, someone knocked on the door. Who could that be? He opened it. Emmy stood there, and damned if his heart didn't thud hard in his chest.

"For you." She held out a foil-covered plate.

"What's this?" he asked, knowing the savory smell meant good food.

"Dinner. Jesse didn't want you to starve."

"My mouth is watering. Tell him thanks."

"I will. He's finishing his math homework, by the way. With no trouble at all, thanks to you. I'll leave you alone now." She turned away.

Mac's stomach wanted that food, and he needed to

finish the mudding. But he wasn't quite ready to let Emmy go. "Tell Jesse I'm proud of him."

She pivoted toward him and nodded, this time, smiling. "He made a friend today, a boy who just moved here."

She looked pleased, years younger. Mac was happy for Jesse and for her. "That's good."

"Isn't it?"

There was nothing more to say, not with words. Emmy's gloved hands fidgeted at her waist. Her eyes collided with Mac's. Tearing his gaze away, he studied the plate. With an appreciative sniff, he lifted the cover. Fragrant steam wafted around him, and he licked his lips.

"It's a chicken-and-rice casserole," Emmy said, also fixed on the plate. "Jess and I pretty much live off casseroles. On weekends I make several and freeze enough to last all week. Saves a lot of time."

"Smart idea. Wish I'd thought of that when I was raising my brothers."

Another awkward silence, the tension between them almost as thick as the caulking mud.

Mac shifted his weight. Cleared his throat. "I'll return the plate when I'm—"

"About last night—" they said at the same time.

Mac set the plate on a pile of cookbooks and beckoned Emmy inside. "It's too cold to have this conversation on the porch."

She crossed the threshold timidly, keeping her hand on the doorknob, looking as if she wanted to bolt and run.

"Last night just happened," Mac said. "I never meant to kiss you and I apologize."

"No need to. I'm not at all sorry." Her eyes widened with surprise and she hastily covered her mouth with her fingers, as if she hadn't meant to admit that.

Mac sure hadn't expected this. "You're not?"

She shook her head. "But it can't happen again."

"Agreed."

Her face was easy to read. Despite her words, she wanted more of what they'd shared. Mac did, too. Needed to pull her close again and finish what they'd started.

Not gonna happen. He grabbed a hammer from the table and weighed it in his hands. "I should get back to work."

"Eat first, before your dinner gets cold."

He intended to. "I'll let you know when I'm ready to go home. Shouldn't be too late."

"Okay." She slipped out the door and closed it softly behind her.

By the time Mac finally finished it was nine-thirty. No doubt by now Jesse must have already gone to bed. The mudding had taken longer than expected, probably because he'd been distracted. The things he wanted to do with Emmy. Kiss her soft lips, touch and taste every inch of her body until she cried out in ecstasy…

His blood simmered, and if his mother had been alive and heard his muttered foul words, she'd have used up a whole bar of soap washing out his mouth.

At least now, after more than twelve hours on the job, he was too worn-out to think about anything. He planned to go home and fall into a dead sleep, safe, if only for tonight, from his ever stronger need for Emmy.

Plate in hand, he crossed the road, his way dimly lit by the streetlight at the end of the cul-de-sac. He walked to Emmy's front stoop. The curtains were closed, but light blazed through the chink between them. He knocked on her door.

A blink later she answered. Soft classical music filled the air. In her hand she clutched a book. Mac couldn't make out the title. He wanted to ask what she was reading, but that would mean having a conversation, which could lead to other things. Especially with her big eyes so warm and those slightly parted lips tempting him.

He thrust out the plate. "Thanks for dinner. It was great. I rinsed the plate off in the bathroom. Sorry I couldn't wash it."

"You're welcome. Gosh, you worked so late, I was starting to wonder whether you'd ever stop." She set the plate and the book down and looked at him like she wanted a repeat of last night.

He did, too, but dammit, he was so not going there. Not tonight. Not ever again. As his hands curled into determined fists, he stared at her shoulder. "Million things to do. I'm ready to go home now."

"Then I'll lock up."

She grabbed her coat. Without waiting for her he strode toward the van, the winter grass crunching under his boots. Standing by the vehicle, he watched her climb the steps and bolt the Rutherfords' door. Then she walked toward him, stopping a foot away.

She tilted her head, the ambient light illuminating her face. Her yearning was clear as day. "Good night, Mac. I'll see you in the morning or if you sleep in, after work."

He started to reach for her, caught himself and jammed his hands into his hip pockets. Hell. Maybe he *would* sleep late, let his brothers start without him. A lot safer that way. "Night, Emmy," he said, sounding gruff to his own ears.

He climbed into the van and locked himself in. Didn't

move or release his breath until she crossed the street to her own yard and closed her door behind her.

As he drove away, he wondered how he'd last the night without going up in flames.

Chapter Nine

By the time Mac cleaned up and ambled into Jim Applebaum's house Friday night, the party was in full swing. Music blared from the CD player and couples crowded the living room, laughing and dancing. Others gathered around the dining-room table, sampling the food and shouting to be heard over the noise. The kind of party Mac's brothers loved.

Mac didn't see anyone over twenty-five. He was probably the oldest guy at the party, which didn't sit well with him. He spotted tall, skinny Jim dancing with a brunette, moved into the man's line of sight and called out a greeting.

"Hey, Mac," Jim replied loudly, flashing a grin while he gyrated to the music. "Long time. Keg's in the kitchen—grab yourself a beer."

Mac hadn't been to a kegger in years. It really wasn't his thing anymore. Wondering if he'd made a mistake coming here but bent on having a good time, he looked for his brothers. They weren't in the living room, but he knew they were around someplace. Probably trolling for single women. At the moment, neither had a girlfriend. Unlike Mac, they each wanted one.

Wandering into the dining room, he nodded at kids he recognized. Caught himself thinking of his brothers' friends as "kids" and snickered. No doubt about it, he definitely felt ancient around this group. College would be like this, too. The thought had him frowning.

Finding a woman here seemed downright pathetic. Keg beer sounded better. Keeping an eye out for Ian and Brian and also checking out the ladies, Mac made his way through the dining room toward the kitchen. Several girls caught his eye, young as they were, and smiled suggestively, and he knew that even if he'd outgrown keggers, even if he felt worlds older, he could pair up with someone tonight and forget about Emmy for a while.

He found his brothers in the kitchen, two of a small bunch congregated around the barrel of beer.

"Hey." He grabbed a plastic glass from a stack on the counter and waited his turn.

Everyone called out hellos, a few with speculative looks. As in, what are *you* doing at this party?

"You made it." Ian saluted.

"We were starting to wonder," Brian said. "Wait'll you taste this beer. It's great, and you could really use a glass or three."

"What's that supposed to mean?" Mac asked, barely able to hear himself over the noise.

"You're way too tense about the remodel job."

"You need to chill out," Ian said. Though the entire house throbbed with conversation, laughter and music, he lowered his voice. "And get laid."

Did his brothers somehow know that lust for Emmy was making his life hell? Mac stiffened. "I haven't been *that* bad."

"No?" Brian said. "Snapping our heads off for any little thing, working twelve-hour days and half of every Saturday? You've been a total pain in the ass."

"Don't hold anything back," Mac muttered.

Ian drained his glass. "We invited you here to relax and hopefully meet someone."

So they hadn't guessed about Emmy. Mac blew out a breath. "And here I thought you wanted more of my pleasant company. Lucky for you, we're on the same wavelength. I'm on the prowl tonight."

At last it was his turn at the keg. He opened the tap and beer frothed into his glass. With his brothers watching, apparently waiting for his opinion, Mac sipped, enjoying the rich flavor. He wiped his mouth with the back of his hand. "Great stuff."

Brian tipped his glass and moved toward the door. "What'd I tell you? Let's head into the dining room, get something to eat and do some babe scoping."

Mac and Ian followed. Standing near the table, they snacked on chips and dip and traded brotherly quips.

"Now you're starting to unwind," Ian said, his attention on a willowy redhead across the way.

"Not bad," Mac said.

"She's a looker, all right. Think I'll ask her to dance."

Brian shrugged. "She's cute, but I have my eye on that girl by the doorway, with the brown, curly hair. What about you, Mac? See anyone interesting?"

Mac glanced around. There were several women with the long legs he favored, but no one in particular grabbed his attention. "Not yet."

"Wish me luck." Ian moved in on the redhead.

"Don't look now, but that blonde with the big rack across the room?" Brian gave a fractional nod toward a small circle of women. "She's looking you over, big brother."

"Yeah?" Mac checked her out. She was small and pretty, and definitely giving him the eye. "Sweet," he murmured.

His brother winked. "Go get her, bro. Later." He made his way toward the woman with the brown curls.

Mac watched his brothers lay on the Struthers charm, and noted they each got a positive response. Seconds later Ian and his new friend headed for the living room to dance. Brian and the curly-haired girl stood to the side, chatting animatedly.

Mac gave them a mental thumbs-up. He hoped they both found whatever it was they wanted tonight. He was sipping his beer, deciding whether to get himself a refill or approach the blonde when the music stopped and she started toward him.

"Hi there," she said, thrusting out her chest. "I'm Christy."

Mac let his gaze flicker over her curves before he nodded. "Mac Struthers."

"It's a *pleasure* to meet you."

She wet her lips, a move meant to rev him up. It didn't. The music started again, a mellow, sultry number.

"Norah Jones—I love this song," Christy said, her eyelids looking heavy. "Would you like to dance?"

A slow dance with a cute, sexy woman was exactly what Mac needed to get things rolling. He smiled. "Love to."

He caught her hand and pulled her into the crowd of dancers. There wasn't much room, but who needed space? She smelled good and felt as soft in his arms as she looked. She was funny, too, cracking jokes. And definitely had the hots for him. Mac knew that if he stuck by her side, she'd let him take her home. But when she snuggled close, he felt nothing beyond mild interest.

What was his problem?

The song seemed to last forever. When it finally ended he pulled away. "Thanks," he said, making no show of asking her for another dance.

"Okay." Christy shrugged and moved on to a different guy.

An hour later his brothers were still with the redhead and the curly-haired girl. While Mac had danced with three different women and chatted up a few more. As attractive as each was, he couldn't summon up much enthusiasm.

Which put him in a lousy mood. He finally nodded good night to his brothers. Their matching incredulous expressions—obviously they couldn't believe he hadn't paired up by now—irked him even more. He thanked Jim and left.

On the drive home he admitted to himself what he'd known deep down for days. There was only one woman he wanted. Emmy Logan. This was not good. Distracted by his troubles, he drove on automatic pilot.

He didn't realize where he was headed until he turned onto Beach Cove Way. Big mistake. He was *not* stopping at Emmy's.

By now she was probably asleep, anyway. He'd turn around in the Rutherfords' driveway and hightail it home.

Only, the lights at her house still glowed through the crack in the drapes. Praying she didn't hear the van, Mac pulled into Tom and Melinda's driveway. As he backed out a loud *pop!* ricocheted through the silence. Mac jumped in his seat. The left front end of the van sagged. Flat tire. He'd probably run over a nail.

Of all the times and places. Cursing his bad luck, he opened the glove box for the flashlight and got out of the van.

After carefully closing the door—he didn't want to make any more noise—he switched on the flashlight. Nothing. Mac shook it. Removed the batteries and reinserted them. The light stayed off. Damned thing was dead.

The porch light didn't exactly illuminate the driveway and the streetlamp at the end of the block was no help. He'd have to change the tire in virtual darkness. Piece of cake.

He had no trouble positioning the jack, hoisting up the vehicle or loosening the lug nuts. But as he began to twist one off with his fingers, his hand slipped. A sharp sting creased the pad of his thumb. Within seconds he was bleeding like a slaughtered pig, and in burning pain.

Having no Band-Aids, tissue or rags to staunch the flow, Mac needed help. He headed for Emmy's.

HUMMING AS SHE washed out the popcorn bowl she and Jess had shared, Emmy realized this was something they hadn't done in ages. Monday was Martin Luther King Day. Eager to begin the long weekend on a fun note, she'd splurged and ordered pizza. She'd also stopped at the grocery for chocolate syrup, sprinkles, whipping cream and cherries for ice-cream sundaes. Then headed for the video store to rent two old favorites, *Transformers* for Jess and *Sleepless in Seattle* for herself. And it *had* been fun, more or less. Jess hadn't exactly opened up. He still hated school and refused to discuss it. Several times he groused about her "lame chick flick," and he fought going to bed. At least he'd spent the entire evening with her, not shut himself in his room. Progress, for sure.

Though by morning that could change. As moody as Jesse was, who knew what the next day would bring?

Now at close to midnight, Emmy was ready to fall into bed herself. She looked forward to sleeping in and enjoying a late, leisurely Saturday morning with a stop at Mocha Java for doughnuts.

Unless Mac showed up, wanting the key. Saturdays, he usually worked for at least some of the day. But with his party tonight, maybe he'd skip tomorrow.

Had he met someone there? Would he go home with her? The very thought dimmed Emmy's mood. Not that she had any hold on Mac Struthers. A few kisses didn't mean a thing, and besides, she didn't have time for romance. The man was leaving soon and wasn't interested in parenting anyone's child. And she refused to ruin what was left of the evening by mooning over him.

As she pulled the plug and the water gurgled from the sink, she heard a loud *pop*. Gunfire? Instantly she froze. But this wasn't Oakland, it was a quiet cul-de-sac on Halo Island. Then again, with most of the houses deserted until summer and the Rutherfords away... Someone might be over there, breaking in. Heart pounding, Emmy hurried to the living room, on the way grabbing the phone to call the police. Clutching it to her chest, she peeked through the drapes.

And jumped. Mac was walking toward her cottage. She darted back.

What was he doing here at this hour?

She set down the phone and quickly smoothed her hair. She opened the door before he knocked. One look at his injured hand and she gasped.

"What happened?"

"Cut the hell out of myself. Do you have a Band-Aid?"

He was bleeding way too much for one little bandage. Judging by the blood, his pale face and taut jaw, he was in pain.

Wincing for him, she widened the door. "I have a first-aid kit. Come in."

"Better give me a rag or a tissue first so I don't drip on your floor."

Considerate even now—how like him. "Wait here."

Emmy grabbed a handful of paper towels. Mac pressed one against the pad of his thumb, then held his hand up to staunch the flow of blood. Despite his cut, he still wiped his feet before he stepped through the door.

"Okay if I use your bathroom?"

"Of course. I'll go with you. You might need me to—"

"I can take care of myself."

Naturally he'd say that. For most of his life he'd been looking after himself and everyone else. He and she were so alike. Equally stubborn, too. She raised her chin. "I'll help you, anyway."

When the mule-headed man opened his mouth to argue, she held a finger to her lips. "Jess is sleeping," she murmured.

Not that anything would bother her son. He always slept like the dead.

She led Mac to the bathroom, which, because tomorrow was cleaning day, wasn't as tidy as she'd have liked. Nothing to be done about that now.

She put the toilet lid down and pushed Mac onto it. He was so big and the room so small that his knees almost brushed the tub. After washing her hands and wetting a clean rag, Emmy leaned over him. Her hair fell forward into her face.

She tried to brush it back with her arm, but that didn't work. To her surprise, Mac tucked it behind her ears with his uninjured hand. It trembled a little. Maybe he was in shock.

"Thanks." She flashed him a quick smile, then began to clean the skin around the wound.

As careful as she was, he flinched.

"Sorry." She bit her lip. "It must really hurt."

His eyes were dark and intent and unsettling. "A little."

Emmy returned her attention to the angry slash. Fresh blood oozed from it, but not as fast and furious as before. Thank goodness.

"The bleeding has slowed," she said. "Have you had a tetanus shot recently?"

"Couple months ago."

"That's good."

With a fresh cloth she lightly blotted the area around the cut. She couldn't help comparing Mac's broad palm to her smaller one. She noted the calluses born of hard, physical labor. His hands were weathered and rough, yet his touch could be so gentle....

Her heart flooded with warmth and tenderness for this man, emotions she couldn't afford and didn't want. Emotions she would hide.

"I don't know, you might need stitches," she said, sparing him only a brief glance.

"I'll be fine."

The stubborn thrust of his jaw warned her not to argue.

"How did this happen?" she asked.

"My tire blew. The flashlight batteries died and I couldn't see what I was doing."

That explained the *pop*. Emmy shook her head. "You couldn't come over and borrow *my* flashlight?"

"I didn't want to bother you so late."

Fine, but that didn't explain why he was in the neighborhood at this hour. Emmy wanted to know. "Aren't you supposed to be at a party?" she asked, instead.

"I was, but I had enough."

That must mean he hadn't met anyone who interested him. Emmy was far too pleased about that. She stood and pulled a roll of sterile gauze and a tube of antibacterial ointment from the bathroom cabinet. Bending down once more, she squeezed the salve onto Mac's wound. Again he tensed and sucked in a breath.

"Time for the bandage." She unrolled the gauze and carefully wrapped it around his thumb and palm.

"You're good at this," he said. "You must have medical training."

Emmy shook her head. "You forget, I'm the mother of a boy. Is there a reason why you parked in the Rutherfords' driveway tonight? Surely you weren't planning to work. If you didn't want to bother me for a flashlight, how would you get the key?"

Mac scowled. "You about finished?"

"Another few seconds." She taped the gauze in place, then brushed her hands together. "All done."

"Thanks. Feels better already."

Mac pushed to his feet. In the tiny room, he was far too close to Emmy. Close enough that she felt his breath on her skin. He smelled of spicy aftershave, beer and fresh air.

His eyes connected with hers, and Emmy forgot about fighting her feelings or hiding them. She forgot everything, even breathing. She finally pulled in a gasp.

Mac's gaze softened, heated. Awareness shivered over her. He cupped her nape with his good hand and lowered his head until his mouth almost brushed hers. With every nerve in her body screaming for his touch and this kiss, she offered her lips.

Mac let out a strangled sound, dropped his hand and backed away, bumping into the wall as if dazed. He spun around and hurried out of the bathroom.

Did he want her or not? Bewildered, Emmy followed him down the hall. She ought to be relieved that Mac had more control than she did. She wasn't.

He was almost at the door. She couldn't let him go, not like this. Neither would she ask him to stay. She had her pride. So she pitched him something entirely different, a proposition he couldn't refuse.

"You can't change your tire with one hand," she said. "I'll help you."

A CERTAIN PART of Mac's frustrated body throbbed painfully. Man, he craved release. He needed to get away from Emmy while he was still able. He hated asking her for help. Bandaging his thumb was enough. But she was right—he couldn't change the flat on his own. At least they'd be outside in the cold night air.

"You ever changed a tire?" he asked.

"No, but you can tell me what to do."

He nodded. "Bring your flashlight."

"Let me scribble a note for Jess first. I don't expect him to wake up, but you never know."

Moments later they stood beside the van, their breaths cloudy in the chill air and a yard of night between them. This was much better. Feeling in control again, Mac took the flashlight from Emmy and aimed the beam at the front tire.

"I already loosened the lug nuts," he said. "You'll need to unscrew them the rest of the way, then give them to me so you don't lose any."

Emmy hunkered down. Her hair was in her face again. Mac thought about brushing it back like he had in the bathroom, but the flowery scent and silky feel of those strands against his skin had nearly undone him. Gripping the flashlight in his good hand, he watched her twist a lug nut and couldn't help imagining those fingers touching a certain part of him, instead.

His groin stirred to life. Angry with himself for going where he shouldn't, he shifted his gaze to the fender. And hoped to God she hurried.

"How're you doing?" he asked, his voice raspy with need.

She didn't seem to notice. "I'm just about… Ta-da! One down."

Smiling and still crouched, she proudly held up the lug nut. Mac stuck the flashlight under his arm as she handed it to him. Her fingers brushed briefly and lightly across his palm. Heat shuddered through him. How sick was that? She was changing a tire, for Chrissake.

He was in one helluva mess here. Looked as if was going to be one of those self-gratification nights. Not Mac's idea of fun, but he had to do *something* to ease this powerful need.

One by one he stowed the lug nuts in his hip pocket until he had all five. Emmy started to jimmy the wheel back and forth to work it off. He stopped her.

"I'm injured, not helpless. I'll do that," he said, taking over.

Now Emmy held the flashlight. Mac removed the flat and laid it on the driveway. He retrieved the spare from the side of the house where he'd leaned it.

The flashlight beam moved over him, and he could feel Emmy's curious gaze.

"What?" he asked.

"It's really cold tonight and you hardly ever wear a jacket," she said, shivering despite her winter coat. "How do you stand it? You must be unusually warm-blooded."

Make that hot. Burning hot. Mac managed a shrug.

"May I put on the new tire?" she asked.

"If you want."

"I do."

She took the spare from him. This time her knuckles skimmed his belly. Mac tensed. So did Emmy, as if she realized she was torturing him. As his body went rock hard, he hissed.

"Mac, I—"

Afraid of what she might say, he jerked his chin at the rim. "Finish with the damn tire, will you?"

She nodded and fit the spare on the wheel. Careful not to touch her, Mac dropped a lug nut into her hand and explained how to spin the nut but not tighten it yet. He directed her to screw on the rest in a diagonal, criss-cross pattern.

"The spare might try to move on you," he cautioned. "I'll hold it in place. When you're through we'll torque everything nice and tight."

At last, mercifully, she finished the job.

"My first tire change. I'm so proud." Emmy brushed her hands on her thighs and beamed. "It was dirty—but fun."

Fun? Try agonizing. Mac stared at her handiwork. "You did a good job. Thanks."

Anxious to leave before he did something he might regret, like kiss her, he loaded the jack and tools into the van, tossed in the flat and slid the door shut.

When he turned around to say goodbye, Emmy stood with her head angled and her expression curious. "I need to know, Mac. Why did you come here tonight?"

How to explain without making a bad situation worse? Mac scrubbed his good hand over his face. "Believe me, I didn't plan this. It just happened. I was turning around in the driveway. I must've run over a nail. You know the rest."

"I'm still confused. Before, when you kissed me… I thought you wanted me." She blushed. "A little while ago… Why did you push me away?"

Mac tried to laugh, but the sound that came out was harsh. "You ask tough questions, know that?"

She didn't say a word, simply waited, and Mac knew he couldn't weasel out of answering her.

"I'm in hell here," he admitted. "I can't stop thinking about you. Tonight I tried, and look where it got me. A flat tire, a gash in my hand. Then what almost happened in the bathroom…" He glanced down at his semihard groin and shook his head. "Like I said, it's hell."

Wondering if he should tell her the rest, he rubbed the space between his eyes. "I want you, Emmy, more than I ever wanted a woman. But being with you that way—it won't work. I can't get involved."

She opened her mouth. Closed it. Then sighed and shut off the flashlight. "I probably shouldn't say this, but talking to you in the dark feels safe, so I'm going to. A month ago, I knew without a doubt that I wasn't ready for any kind of relationship. I also realized that when the time felt right, I wanted a commitment from a man willing to stick around and help raise Jesse. But now, with you…"

Pausing a moment, she wrapped her arms around her waist. "I want you as badly as you want me. And I'm beginning to think that sex with no strings is okay."

Even in the scant light her eyes glittered with feeling, with need. It would be easy to reach for her and indulge in the pleasure and sexual release they both yearned for. And so good.

Mac blew out a breath as clouded as his reasoning. "I know you, Emmy, and no matter what you feel right now, sex isn't enough for you. You need a man to love you and, like you said, be a father to Jesse. Things I can't give you. I'm afraid you'd… I don't want to hurt you."

Her chin jutted. "I'm not some fragile little flower, Mac. I can take care of myself. I always have."

Mac had no doubt of that, but still wasn't convinced. "You'd better think carefully about this, make sure that sex and only sex is what you want."

"I meant what I said. It is."

Despite her level gaze, his gut told him she needed space and time to decide. So did he. "All the same, I'll feel better if you think about it some more."

She rolled her eyes in a gesture reminiscent of her son. "All right."

That was a relief. "With my bum thumb, I'm taking the whole weekend off," he said. "I won't be back until Monday."

"I'll let you know my decision then."

"Take longer if you need to."

She nodded.

"Would you mind not telling anyone about tonight?"

Mac said. "If my brothers found out I was here…" They'd have a field day with this.

Emmy pretended to lock her lips. "I won't. You'd be surprised at the secrets I'm keeping."

While Mac mulled over that interesting statement, wondering who'd confided in her, she gave him a sweet smile. "Won't Brian and Ian wonder how you hurt your hand?"

"I'll say the tire blowout happened on the way home. Night, Emmy."

"Good night."

She touched her fingers to her lips, then pressed them to his mouth, leaving him burning for the real thing. He didn't hide his need as he kissed her fingertips.

Neither of them saw Jesse watching through a chink in the living-room drapes.

Chapter Ten

Jesse awoke with a start. Barely conscious, rubbing his eyes, he padded into the living room, blinking in the light from the reading lamp. A note from his mom lay on the coffee table. *I'm next door at the Rutherfords'—back soon.*

More alert now, he glanced at the clock in the kitchen. Ten after twelve. Mom didn't go out much at night, especially this late. What was she doing over there?

Curious, he peered through the slit between the drapes. There wasn't much light across the street, but he saw Mac's van in the driveway. He always parked out front, so this was different. He was standing next to the vehicle with his mom, and she was touching his mouth with her hand. Sometimes she did that to Jesse—a kiss with fingers, instead of lips. By the way she kept her eyes on Mac's face and the tilt of Mac's head toward her, Jesse knew they were starting to be more than just friends.

His mom never said anything, but he guessed she was lonely. Mac was the first guy she'd liked since Dad left. He was cool, and he knew how to do math homework.

"Awesome," Jesse whispered.

His mom dropped her hand and Mac stepped into the van's shadow. She turned away and headed toward their house. Jesse didn't want her to catch him awake. Giddy from his discovery, he giggled and hightailed it back to bed. He heard her come inside, shut the door and dead-bolt it. Her coat swished as she slipped out of it and hung it up.

Certain that she'd peek in to check on him like she always did, he forced himself to lie still and fake sleep.

Sure enough, seconds later his bedroom door creaked open. Jesse kept his eyes screwed tight and breathed slowly. When she closed the door and he knew she was gone, he smiled in the darkness.

Mac and his mom together would be so great. He might stay here, instead of leaving. Maybe. *If* Jesse didn't screw things up. Like he had with his dad.

His smile faded. He still remembered when his father had walked out just before Valentine's Day. Jesse remembered this because it was the morning he'd cut out hearts at kindergarten and made cards for his parents. That afternoon his dad, who usually got home at dinnertime, arrived early. He was in a really bad mood. The babysitter left. Saying he needed space, Jesse's dad sent him outside to play with Corry, his friend across the street. Jesse remembered tossing a baseball back and forth with Corry, the way some of the older guys did. They were only five, and not very good at throwing or catching. Jesse missed a ball from Corry. It sailed over his head and hit the hood of his dad's car. The impact left a ding on the shiny black surface.

His dad must've been watching. He came out yelling and cursing something awful. Corry ran home, crying, and Jesse's dad stomped inside again. Humiliated and ashamed for missing the ball and putting a dent in the car, Jess had sprinted to a nearby tree, climbed up and stayed there until he figured out how to make things right. Then he shinnied down and quietly crept to his room.

He opened his piggy bank and tipped out all the money he was collecting to buy a bicycle. It was too much for him to count. There were so many coins and dollar bills, he couldn't carry them all in his hands. So he put them back into the bank.

He heard his mother drive up, but instead of hurrying to welcome her, he brought the piggy bank to his parents' bedroom, where his dad was packing two suitcases.

"What's this?" he asked when Jess handed over his savings.

"It's to pay for fixing the ding."

His father had laughed in a way that sounded more like he was angry. "Don't be ridiculous. All the money in the world won't make me stay here."

It was the last thing he said before he snapped the bags closed, hefted them and strode outside to meet Jesse's mom.

After all this time, Jesse's conscience still hurt from what he'd done. Driven his father away.

He hugged his pillow and made a silent vow. This time things would be different. He was through acting up. From now on, he'd be extra good and extra nice. Then surely, Mac would stick around.

MONDAY MORNING, at the end of a three-day weekend spent cleaning, cooking, freezing meals and running errands, Emmy sat on the sofa folding laundry. Jesse was at the kitchen table, finishing his homework with barely a mumble. For no reason she knew of, starting with their doughnut breakfast at Mocha Java Saturday morning, her surly son had turned into a sunny, enjoyable child. He'd stayed that way all weekend, unusually cooperative, cleaning his room and doing whatever else she asked of him without a single argument. He'd even offered to wash the dishes after she baked cookies and brownies for the week.

The sudden shift in attitude more than surprised her and made her wonder what had happened to cause it. As Emmy folded a pair of her son's jeans she resisted the urge to ask the universe what it'd done with the Jesse she knew. She was too pleased to question this wonderful change.

Today the sun actually shone, though weakly, as if it approved of this new, improved boy. Cold as it was, it was a perfect day to explore the beach together. At least worth a suggestion. So far Jess had declined. Now, though…

Emmy smiled to herself. Her son still needed a friend. She'd suggest inviting Peter, the boy from the library, over to walk the beach with them. Or anything else Jess wanted to do, as long as part of the day included the two of them. Preferably something away from the house. From Mac.

The man she couldn't stop thinking about was across the street, only a few dozen feet away. Far too close. Hoping for a glimpse of him, Emmy glanced out the window. Caught herself and turned her attention to pairing up socks. The darned man had filled her thoughts all weekend. Did his thumb hurt and had he stopped at the emergency room, after all? Mostly though, Emmy had mulled over their conversation Friday night, seriously considering what she wanted from Mac. The truth was, she was already half in love with him, which, given that he was leaving and wasn't looking for a real relationship, was beyond foolish. He certainly wasn't lining up to be anyone's father, either.

Even so, Emmy hadn't changed her mind. She ached for him so much she could barely focus on anything else. The only way to find peace and get on with her life was to give in to the passion.

She'd planned to tell Mac when she'd unlocked the Rutherfords' door this morning, long before Jess awoke. Not the part about falling for him, but that she wanted and needed to be with him sexually for the few short weeks before he left. Only, his brothers had shown up just when Mac had, and there'd been no chance to speak openly. Worse, she'd had to pretend surprise at his injury.

Emmy hoped to talk with Mac tonight when she locked up—unless Jess came along. If so, she'd call him after Jess went to bed.

She heard her son's schoolbook plop closed and the scrape of the kitchen chair as he pushed away from the table. She looked up and saw him standing in the space separating the kitchen and living room. His hair stuck out in places, and Emmy knew he'd raked his hands through it while he worked. She itched to go over to him and smooth it down, but wasn't sure the new, agreeable Jess would tolerate that any more than before.

So she smoothed a freshly folded T-shirt, instead. "Done already?"

He nodded. "Will you quiz me on my spelling later?"

How long had it been since he'd asked her to do that? A good year, at least. "I'd love to," she said, again marveling at—and curious about—this sudden attitude change. "I'm about finished, too. It's such a pretty day. How would you like to explore the beach with me? You could call Peter and invite him along."

"Umm…" Jesse dipped his head and shifted his weight. "I kind of wanted to hang out with Mac and his brothers."

Worried about Jess making a nuisance of himself, Emmy smiled apologetically. "They're really busy, Jesse. Maybe later this afternoon." She handed her son his laundry. "Please put these things away."

"But, Mo-om. I haven't been over there since Friday."

Never mind that the Struthers men had taken the weekend off. Emmy shook her head. "I really think—"

"At least let me bring them some of those brownies you baked yesterday. You know how much Mac loves chocolate."

Her son almost sounded as if he somehow realized the depth of Emmy's feelings for Mac. But no, no one knew. She squinted at her eager-faced boy. "Exactly what are you getting at?"

He shrugged. "Mac and his brothers work so hard, even on Martin Luther King Day. Sometimes when I have a lot to do you give me treats. Can I please take over some brownies after I put my clothes away? Then I'll go to the beach with you."

"*May* I," Emmy corrected.

"May I?" Jess gave her the round-eyed, pleading, puppy-dog look she couldn't resist. He was absolutely right. Mac, Ian and Brian all had a sweet tooth. They'd certainly wolfed down her cookies after dinner the other night. They'd probably enjoy home-baked brownies.

"All right, I'll cut them some brownies and you can take them over," she said. "But only if you come straight home again. I expect you back in fifteen minutes."

"I have an idea," Jesse said. "Why don't you come get me when you're ready to go down to the beach?"

The funny feeling in Emmy's stomach whispered that he was up to something. She narrowed her eyes. Her son looked puzzled and perfectly innocent, so she dismissed her misgivings.

Not wanting to see Mac again this morning, she shook her head. "I'll wait for you here, instead. Remember, fifteen minutes."

TIM MCGRAW SANG a plaintive song on the portable radio, good for a morning break. Mac poured himself a cup of lukewarm coffee from his jumbo thermos, then sat down on the unstained oak floor, joining Ian and Brian.

Ian whipped out his iPhone and started texting. Brian pulled a book from his back pocket, some nonfiction thing on communication on the Internet. Even though he was through school, he continued to read up on computers. He was quite the geek.

But he didn't open the book; instead, he nodded at Mac's bandage. "How's that thumb feeling?"

Sore as hell, Mac's penance for driving over here Friday night. For wanting Emmy and for what he'd said to her. For—

"Mac?" Ian waved his hand in front of Mac's face. "Your thumb?"

"Right. Not bad if I'm careful."

"Cool." Ian finished texting and yawned.

"If you don't quit with the yawning, you're gonna get me doing it," Brian said. "Pour yourself some coffee."

"You're just jealous. I can't help it if Rebecca and I hit it off." Grinning, Ian reached for the thermos.

The girl from the party, according to Ian. And he'd talked a lot about her this morning—they'd spent most of the weekend together.

"Is that who you texted?" Mac asked.

Ian nodded.

"Maybe I don't move as fast as you," Brian said. "That doesn't mean I struck out. FYI, I called Bethany a little while ago. We're going to dinner and a movie tomorrow night."

Mac's brothers high-fived each other.

He listened idly as they discussed what they wanted and hoped for with their new girlfriends. Truth was, he envied them. Their lives were relatively simple. Meet a woman, date her and see where things led.

Whereas his was far more complicated. Even if he wanted to—and he didn't—he couldn't get involved with Emmy. Not unless a short-term, sex-only relationship worked for her. From her expression this morning, Mac knew she wanted to share her decision with him. He was eager to do just that, but with his brothers showing up when they did, it hadn't been possible.

"Too bad you didn't meet someone at the party, Mac."

If his brothers only knew. Not about to share what had happened between him and Emmy—if anything really had—Mac shrugged. "Luck of the draw."

"I thought for sure you and that blonde would hit it off," Brian said. "If you had, maybe you wouldn't have sliced your thumb."

He wouldn't have had that frank talk with Emmy, either. Or spent the weekend a physical wreck. Thinking about her, wanting her, waiting for today. Then not being able to talk alone.

Hell. If they couldn't even *talk* privately, how would they find a time and place to have sex?

"Mac? You're a million miles away. Again."

"Guess I was. I've been thinking about whether to install the sink first or—"

A forceful knock interrupted him. Emmy?

His gut tight with anticipation, Mac cleared his throat. "I'll get that." He scrambled up. "We should get back to work soon, so finish your drinks."

He set his cup aside. Then as excited as a kid on his birthday, he made his way through the narrow clearing toward the front door. He glanced out the window and saw Jesse out there. No sign of his mother.

Disappointed but also relieved, Mac glanced over his shoulder. His brothers had followed him. "It's Jesse."

"Wondered when he'd show up," Ian said. "Since there's no school today."

"Emmy's at home, too. Maybe she'll ask us to dinner tonight." Brian rubbed his stomach. "Too bad you have a date, Ian."

Wondering if Jess was here to invite them over and not sure he should accept, Mac opened the door. "Hey there."

"Hi."

The boy clutched a foil packet that smelled of chocolate. Mac and his brothers eyed it with interest.

"What's in there?" Ian asked.

Brian sniffed. "Brownies?"

"How'd you guess?" Jesse glanced at Mac and frowned. "What happened to your thumb?"

"I cut it changing a flat tire in the dark."

"Oh. Was that when…" Flushing, the boy broke off.

Did he know about the other night? "When what?" Mac said, bracing for whatever came next.

"Never mind. I promised my mom I'd be back in fifteen minutes, so I can't stay long." Jess held out the package to Mac like an offering. "These are from my mom, and they're really good."

The boy didn't know anything, just wanted to give them the brownies. Mac relaxed.

"Are they just for Mac, or do we get some, too?" Brian asked, sending a speculative look Mac's way.

"They're for all of you," Jesse said. "She put in six— that's two each. Go ahead, try one."

"You don't have to ask twice." Mouth watering, Mac picked up a brownie, then passed the rest to his brothers. He bit into the moist cake and chewed with relish. "She made these from scratch, huh? Delicious."

"Your mom makes the best desserts," Ian added around a mouthful.

Brian polished off his brownie in two bites and reached for another. "Tell her thanks."

"Okay."

Jesse glanced at Mac with a questioning expression. He seemed to expect something more from Mac, but for the life of him, Mac couldn't figure out what.

READY TO LOCK UP, Emmy stood with Mac on the porch. Beyond the yellow halo of light, darkness surrounded them and rain tattooed softly on the eaves. Cozy, but cold, and she was glad she'd pulled on gloves and a scarf.

"The weirdest thing," she said. "Jess didn't want to come over here with me tonight. He said he'd rather take a shower, then watch TV."

Give up the opportunity to say good-night to Mac? He'd never done that before. Puzzling, and coupled with his new model-son behavior, troubling.

Mac shrugged. "He was here earlier. Maybe that was enough. Thanks for the brownies, by the way. They were great. I could've eaten a dozen."

He patted his stomach and smacked his lips, and Emmy laughed. "I'll keep that in mind. You should thank Jesse. It was his idea."

"Yeah?" Mac grinned. "Any time he wants to bring over more is fine with me."

"I'll tell him," Emmy said, but she couldn't summon a smile. She was too worried. "Did he seem strange to you?"

"How so?"

"He's been different all weekend. Cooperative and helpful without my asking."

"And that's bad?"

"I'm not sure. It's certainly unusual."

"Now there's a twist." Mac's mouth quirked. "Last week you wondered if you two would always argue. Now you're upset that you're getting along."

"I know, but…" Trying to put her feelings into words, Emmy thought a moment. "Something feels off."

"He seemed okay to me." Mac sat down on the sheltered top step and patted the space next to him. "Tell me what you're worried about."

He looked ready to listen, and Emmy was grateful. She needed to talk to someone who understood kids.

She sat down beside him, the step cold and hard beneath her. "I wish I could explain. Friday night he went to bed happy about the three-day weekend, but still his normal, argumentative self. Saturday morning he walked into the kitchen a different boy. After he brought you the brownies this morning, we explored the beach together. I wanted him to invite his friend, Peter, but he said he'd rather hang out with me. Yet when I mentioned walking the beach last weekend, he snorted and shut himself in his room. On the way home we shopped for fabric for new kitchen curtains. Jess *hates* waiting around in a fabric store, yet today he never said one negative word."

Cold despite her coat, Emmy shivered. "Everything I suggested, he agreed to. It's almost as if he's afraid that if he argues with me, something bad will happen."

Mac started to rub his chin with his forefinger and injured thumb. Wincing, he instead rested his hand on his thigh. "I never dealt with anything like that. I'm stymied."

"Do you think he knows something about us?"

"How could he? There's nothing to know—yet."

Leaning back, resting his elbows on the porch floor, he angled his chin in unspoken question. Silently asking for Emmy's decision.

More than ready to tell him, she didn't hesitate. "Over the weekend I thought a lot about us."

"And?" His gaze fastened on her.

"I haven't changed my mind from the other night. I still want to go to bed with you."

His eyes went dark and hot. He sat up straight. "How are we going to work this?"

"I don't know, but Jesse can't find out. He can't even *wonder.* I don't want him thinking we're starting a long-term relationship and then wind up getting hurt."

"I'm with you a hundred percent." Mac glanced at her mouth. "Do you have to get back right away?"

For once his expression was easy to read. He wanted to be alone with her *now.*

Emmy wanted that, too. Heart pounding, she shook her head. "By now Jess should be in the shower. He usually stays there a good half hour."

Mac nodded. "It's cold out here." He stood and grabbed her hand. "Why don't you come inside and warm up."

Trembling, Emmy unlocked the door she'd just dead-bolted. In the living room she shouldered out of her coat.

The drapes were closed and except for a small table

lamp that stayed on all night, the rest of the house was dark. Despite the jumble of kitchen items, the room felt private and even romantic.

The instant Mac closed the door he pulled Emmy close and kissed her.

Chapter Eleven

Emmy tasted sweeter than her brownies, all soft and warm and willing. Her breasts pressed into his chest and her hips molded to his. A great start, but not nearly enough.

Hungry for more, Mac coaxed her lips apart and plunged his tongue into her mouth, mimicking what he really wanted, to get inside her. She responded eagerly, her own tongue restless. She wriggled closer, her hip shimmy teasing him. Killing him. His groin jumped to life, hard and demanding.

Mac groaned and clasped her butt. He couldn't get enough of her. He backed her up to the wall. Hooked her leg around his so that the most sensitive part of her was open to him. Or would be without the jeans and panties. He ground against her, pleasing them both. Emmy made a sound of enjoyment, tightened her thigh around him and pulled herself closer still.

If he didn't touch her now, he'd seriously go into shock. He slid his hands under her sweater. Her warm skin was taut and smooth.

Watching her through heavy-lidded eyes, he cupped her breasts through her bra, registering the weight and fullness. With a breathy sound she thrust her chest forward. Mac skimmed his nails over her nipples. Instantly they sharpened and she let her head loll against the wall.

"Oh, Mac," she whispered. "That feels…"

"Really good?" He stroked again, watching her face open to the sensation.

"Yes." She strung the word out in a hiss of pleasure.

Her enjoyment was a real turn-on. "This sweater must go," he said, tugging the hem upward.

Emmy raised her arms over her head. Mac pulled the sweater off and tossed it aside.

"Now you," she said.

Blood roaring in his ears, he shed his T-shirt in record time.

Her face and neck were flushed with desire, and her nipples prodded the cups of her bra. This one hooked in front. Her eyes locked on him, Emmy unfastened the clasp and slid the straps down. The bra fell away.

Her breasts were round and heavy, with large, dusky nipples peaked with desire. For him. Mac swallowed past a wave of feeling he couldn't define. "You are beautiful."

Impatient to taste her, he flicked each nipple with his tongue. She quivered and he licked again, then gently suckled and teased each breast until she squirmed and gripped his shoulders hard.

"My legs… I need to sit down," she said, all breathy again.

Mac glanced at the plastic-covered furniture, all of it piled with kitchen stuff. There was only the floor of the skinny aisle between the door and kitchen, and it was dirty and uncomfortable.

"No place to sit," he said. Clasping her waist, he lifted her. "Wrap your legs around me."

"I'm not too heavy?"

"No." Lowering his head, he again pleasured her breasts with his mouth.

"Dear God," Emmy moaned, restlessly shifting. "I want to make love with you now."

What that did to him! He raised his head. "Help me with your jeans."

The snap popped. He jerked the zipper open. Emmy eased back to give him access. Too bad they weren't lying down, but this was better than nothing.

With his good hand he dipped under the elastic of her panties. Slid his fingers into her soft thatch, all the while watching her.

Her eyes were closed and her lips slightly open. Need colored her expression and passion flushed her skin. She was the most beautiful woman Mac had ever known. Feelings he didn't understand or want filled his chest. Spooked, he hesitated. What the hell was he doing?

"Please don't stop," Emmy whispered, raising her hips and squeezing her legs tight.

The way she was positioned, Mac couldn't slip his fingers inside her. But he could reach the tiny, wet nub. He'd barely touched it before she gasped and came undone.

No woman he'd been with had ever climaxed so quickly. He almost went over the edge with her. Somehow he held back.

When her frenzy finally ended, she gazed up at him with limpid wonder. "Thank you."

"My pleasure." And it had been. Even though Mac was hard and aching, almost wild to strip off the rest of their clothes and bury himself in her, for now pleasuring Emmy was enough.

She unhooked her legs, slid to the floor and fastened her jeans. Mac backed up shakily.

"I've never come that way before," she said, covering her breasts with her arms. "Not with a man."

Not with a— *Whoa.* "You're saying you like women?"

"No." She blushed. "What I mean is, um, from time to time, I use a vibrator."

An activity Mac wouldn't mind watching. And he had to know. "How long since you've been with a man?"

"A very long time. Since Chas left."

That explained plenty. That she'd chosen Mac after all this time meant a lot. He touched her cheek. "It's been a while for me, too."

Pleasuring Emmy for the next few weeks was going to be great.

Shielding her breasts with one arm, she slid her palm down his belly, straight to his erection.

Sweet heaven. Mac gritted his teeth. "Don't." Catching hold of her wrist, he lifted her hand. "Or I'll embarrass myself."

"But that's not fair to you." She stared pointedly at his strained fly. "You need release, too."

"Another time. We've been here a long while. Jesse's probably through showering. You'd best go." He retrieved her bra and sweater and handed them to her. She turned away to dress. Mac tugged on his T-shirt.

"When are we going to be together the way we want—naked and in bed?" he asked.

Clothed now, she faced him and finger-combed her hair. "I don't know. Soon, I hope. We need a place to go where we can be alone for more than thirty minutes."

Mac was with her there. "How about one of these empty bedrooms?"

"In the Rutherfords' house?" She looked horrified. "I'd never be able to look them in the face again."

"We sure can't use your cottage, not with Jesse around." Mac brushed her hair off her face and anchored it behind her ears.

She closed her eyes. Her lips parted. With a soft sigh she leaned into his palm, and he knew that if he wanted to, he could fire her up again. Though he burned with need to take her here and now, she was right. This wasn't the place. When he and Emmy made love, they'd do it in a bed, taking their sweet time. He dropped his hand and she opened her eyes.

"I wish I could come to your house," she said. "But I don't feel right leaving Jess alone yet. Besides, where would I tell him I was going?"

"Good point." At a loss, Mac scratched the back of his neck.

"What about the van?" Emmy asked.

As badly as he wanted her, he wasn't about to make love to her there. He shook his head. "You deserve better than that."

"Where doesn't matter. As long as we're together."

Her honesty and need were as potent as a touch. Mac groaned. "This is worse than being a teenager." He helped Emmy into her coat. "All hot and bothered with no place to go."

"We'll figure it out." She fastened the top button. "Do I look all right?"

With her lips kiss-swollen, her cheeks pink and her eyes dark and luminous, she looked amazing. But she was worried about her son. "You're fine," Mac said. "Jesse won't know what we've been doing."

She nodded and they stepped through the door and

onto the porch. Emmy locked the dead bolt. After shooting Mac a quick smile, she hurried down the steps. He stayed put until she ducked into her house. Then aching but oddly satisfied, he headed for the van.

FRIDAY AFTERNOON Emmy sat at her desk, logging in this week's new library books. Normally she enjoyed flipping through them and deciding which ones she wanted to read. Today she was too distracted. For the past two weeks, while Jesse showered before bed, she'd met Mac at the Rutherfords' for passionate kisses and hurried caresses.

Emmy lived for those stolen moments together, her desire for Mac—and her feelings—growing with each embrace. Her body hummed and ached for his attention, and his skilled hands and mouth showed her glimpses of heaven. But no matter how sweet Mac's touch was, she craved more. If they didn't find a place to make love soon, she just might pop out of her skin.

While she printed out a book label with the library's bar code, she let out a sigh of longing, just as Sally passed by.

The woman stopped and glanced curiously at Emmy. "My, that sounded weighty."

"Guess I was daydreaming," Emmy said.

"Not in a good way, though. Do you want to talk about it?"

At her encouraging smile, Emmy considered sharing her problems. She could do with some motherly advice. But what would she say? That each day she loved Mac a little more? That she dreamed of him as a permanent part of her life, even though that wasn't possible, that when he left it was going to hurt, but that right now, she was too involved, too needy, to care? Not about to admit her weaknesses to Sally—she'd sound like an utter fool—Emmy smoothed the bar-code label over the book's spine.

"I'm fine, really," she said. "A little sleep-deprived, that's all." Wound up from Mac's kisses and touches and frustrated and aching for more, she slept restlessly, waking often. She was sick to death of sneaking around. Like teenagers, Mac said. Would they ever spend a night together and make love? "I'm sure I'll catch up this weekend." With the help of one of those p.m. pain relievers that make you drowsy.

"TGIF, huh?"

"Something like that."

"It's been a darned good week, though, hasn't it? Your after-school program is off to a great start."

True, and something to be grateful for. Emmy smiled. "I'm pleased."

Patty, whose shift had started a short while earlier, joined Sally in front of Emmy's desk. "You should be. The children will love what you lined up for today. Ian and Brian Struthers. I wish I could participate. Unfortunately someone has to stay out here and work." She glanced at Sally and smiled. "And since you're going home soon…"

"Dinner date with my husband," Sally said. "Or I'd stay late. I am planning to peek in, though. The men discussing remodeling and construction, then sharing some of their portable tools—what a treat for the kids."

Earlier in the week, between fevered kisses, Emmy had convinced Mac that he could spare Brian and Ian for one afternoon. She glanced at the round wall clock. "It's after three. Brian and Ian should be here any minute."

As if her words had summoned them, the brothers pushed through the door with a toolbox, a bag of safety glasses and a large canvas tarp. Emmy hurried to meet them.

"Hey, Emmy." Ian grinned.

"Where do you want this stuff?" Brian asked.

"Follow me." She led them into the meeting room, where she hosted the after-school program.

"Nice space." Ian set down his load.

Brian followed suit. "When we were kids and came to the library, we never had a room to ourselves. We were always getting shushed for not keeping our voices down."

"Not in here," Emmy said. "Once we shut the door, the kids are free to make as much noise as they want."

Ian stroked his goatee and eyed the rectangular tables and folding chairs. "Be a shame to ruin this nice blue carpet. Let's lay down the tarp. Then we'll bring in the rest of our tools."

As always he was careful of not making a mess. Just like Mac. Emmy smiled. "Great idea."

They dragged the chairs and tables out of the way, Ian and Brian teasing each other.

"You're lucky we're here." Ian unfolded the tarp. "We hit a few snafus this morning and got a little behind. Mac was a real pri— Bear."

"Yeah, but he's been that way for weeks now."

"You're so right, bro, but it was worse today."

Brian's mouth quirked as he helped Ian spread out the canvas. "I think he's jealous that he wasn't invited this afternoon."

The brothers lifted the tables and repositioned them atop the tarp, then helped Emmy arrange the folding chairs.

"He said he couldn't spare the time," she said.

"I know, but I think he changed his mind," Brian said. "Better he stayed behind than us, since he's the only Struthers man who enjoys the work."

Ian shot his twin a dirty look and shoved two chairs under a table. "What're you doing, sharing our private stuff?"

"Emmy knows. I told her weeks ago. She promised not to say anything to Mac. Right, Emmy?"

Both men looked at her.

She nodded and with her finger drew a cross over her heart. And felt a pang of guilt. Mac ought to be told that his brothers wanted their own, different careers. "If it were me, I'd explain it to him," she said. "But a promise is a promise and, anyway, it's not my place."

"You like him a lot, don't you?" Ian said.

Emmy's cheeks warmed and she knew she was blushing. She ducked her head to position a chair.

"She does!" Brian chuckled. "He likes you, too."

Emmy wondered at his cagey look. Had he guessed about them? Of course not. They were too careful.

Suddenly the door opened, saving her from more teasing.

Sally stuck her head in. "The school bus just pulled onto our street."

Emmy nodded. "Thanks. That gives us about three minutes."

"Whoa," Brian said. "We'd best grab the rest of our tools from the truck."

The two men strode out and Emmy sagged with relief. They made her nervous with their talk about her and Mac caring for each other. Mainly because it was true. And because she worried that Jesse might find out. In the end, her son would only get hurt, and he'd suffered enough.

MORE THAN A DOZEN kids from grade and middle school poured into the meeting room, Jesse and Peter among the last. While Emmy greeted every child, she sneaked a glimpse at Jess. His face was far too sober—he still rarely smiled—but solemn was better than sullen defiance. For that she was grateful. Nearly two weeks had passed since his attitude had done a U-turn, and she no longer cared why. She suspected that Peter, whose sunny disposition and warm smile brightened every room, was partly responsible. Undoubtedly influenced by his friend's attitude, Jesse no longer complained about school or dragged his feet over coming to the library every afternoon. He'd also stopped whining about moving back to Oakland.

Emmy knew that moving here was her smartest decision ever. Even if she ended up with a broken heart later. But she wouldn't worry about Mac or the future now.

She greeted Jesse and Peter with a smile. "Hey, you two."

Peter beamed. "Hi, Ms. Logan."

"How was school?" she asked Jesse.

"Okay. Where are Ian and Brian?"

"Getting their gear from the truck. While we're waiting, go ahead and find seats." She raised her voice to include all the children. "If you brought a snack, hurry and eat, because once Brian and Ian start their program, you'll want to give them your full attention."

A few minutes later the men shouldered through the

door, biceps bulging as they each hefted several portable tools. Emmy moved to the back of the room and closed the door behind them. As she followed them forward, all eyes fixed on the handsome twins.

They saw Jesse and greeted him warmly. Emmy's son sat up straight and at last grinned, a beaming show of teeth that warmed the afternoon like the summer sun and brought out her own appreciative smile.

After the twins laid out their tools on the floor, Emmy introduced them. "Today we have a real treat. Brian and Ian Struthers will tell us about construction and teach us how to handle some of the tools they use every day. Let's welcome them."

Enthusiastic applause and a few boyish yahoos—the girls were quieter—filled the air. The door opened and Sally stepped into the room. Staying at the back of the room, she waved at the men.

Ian began. "I'm Ian, and that's my twin brother, Brian. Like Emmy—Ms. Logan—said, we're in the construction business. Actually the work we do is called renovation or remodeling. That means we tear down the old and build a newer version. We work on houses, but some people remodel commercial buildings. Before we go on, you should know that Brian and I are in this library all the time."

"But you're grown-ups," said Creighton, a pimple-faced, preteen boy, his voice cracking.

"That we are," Brian said. "Libraries are for everyone, not just kids."

"When we *were* kids, though, we spent every afternoon in here, doing our homework and enjoying the after-school programs." Ian gestured at everyone. "Just like you."

Every child looked delighted. Emmy bit back a smile. Ian and Brian were naturals with kids.

"We brought some of our tools," Brian said. "We're about to show you how they work and teach you how to operate them. But first, who has questions?" Several hands shot up. "Girl with the pigtails."

"That's April," Emmy told him.

One of two first graders, April smiled, showing a gap where her two front teeth should be. "Do you like remodeling?"

Only Emmy detected the slight hesitation. Both men nodded.

"Sometimes there are challenges along the way," Ian said. "But the end results make any problems worth the effort." He called on a pudgy eight-year-old boy.

"How did you get started?"

The twins traded looks, and Brian answered the question. "Our older brother, Mac, launched the business. He's leaving the island in about two weeks, though, to travel and then go to college. While he's gone, we'll take over."

For a moment Jesse looked startled, as if he'd forgotten about Mac leaving. Then a smug, knowing look flickered across his face. Emmy had no idea what he was thinking. And at the moment, no time to wonder.

"You mean your big brother hasn't gone to college yet?" asked a rail-thin, blushing seventh-grade girl.

Brian shook his head. "Hasn't had the time. But he knows the importance of an education, and he's bound and determined to get himself a degree."

"Did you go to school?" fifteen-year old Will asked.

Brian nodded. "Ian and I both did."

"Do you need to go to college if you remodel houses?" Will asked.

"Not really, but you can't go wrong with an education."

"We should probably move on now," Emmy said. "If there's time later, people can ask more questions." She moved to the side of the room, out of the way.

Brian held up a black drill. "Anyone know what this is?"

Jesse's hand was the first up. Ian nodded at him. "Jesse?"

"That's an electric drill. I got to try it the other day. That's because I live across the street from where Mac and Ian and Brian are working, so I get to hang out with them sometimes," he added with obvious pride.

Several of the kids, including Peter, oohed and ahhed with admiration, and Emmy's son puffed out his chest. Emmy felt just as proud, and happy for him.

Ian and Brian discussed safety, then donned eye protection. They showed how to change the drill bit and demonstrated turning the motor on and off.

"Now it's your turn," Ian said, looking slightly bug-eyed in the glasses. "We brought two drills today and enough safety goggles for everyone. You'll get to keep those."

"Cool," someone said.

"Brian and I will each work with one person at a time," Ian went on. "Who wants to try first?"

Every hand shot up. Sally waved goodbye to Emmy and slipped out.

For the next hour the men showed off various tools and let the kids operate them. Time flew by, and everyone was surprised when the parents began to arrive.

Most of the adults seemed impressed and a bit

envious that they'd missed the presentation. Some chatted with Ian and Brian and asked for their cards in case they had remodeling work to be done in the future.

Soon all the children except Peter and Jesse had gone. The two boys and Emmy helped Brian and Ian toss the wood scraps they'd brought into the trash and fold the tarp.

"That was a terrific program," Emmy said. "I'd love for you to came back again. Maybe in a few months?"

Ian fiddled with his mustache. "That'd be cool. I'd like to talk about computer programming."

"Put me down for media communications," Brian said. "But not until winter. Summer and fall are real busy times for us."

Ian nodded. "Especially with Mac gone. Besides being swamped with jobs, we'll still be adjusting to running the business. We'll probably contract out some of the work Mac usually does, but I'm betting on much longer hours for us."

Ian nodded. "It's all up in the air right now. Could we schedule a date later in the year?"

They weren't the only ones who'd need time to adjust to life without Mac. Emmy certainly would. She dreaded dealing with the pain and loneliness, dreaded helping her son do the same. Though at the moment, instead of looking sad or upset that the man he so looked up to would soon leave, her son wore a complacent smile. It was the second occasion this afternoon that his expression was at odds with what she expected.

How strange. She made a mental note to talk with him later and make certain he understood that Mac would be gone for several years. She'd ask Mac to do the same. Again.

As soon as the door shut behind the men, Jesse turned to Emmy. "Can I spend the night at Peter's?"

"May I."

"May I?"

He tried to tamp down his eagerness, which was so like him. Was this why Mac's leaving town didn't bother him, because he was so involved with Peter? Emmy hoped so.

"Mom?"

"That depends," she said. "Peter, have you checked with your parents?"

"I'm gonna when my mom comes to pick me up."

This first invitation to his friend's house delighted Emmy. And meant she'd have the cottage to herself the whole evening. Mac could stay the night. Finally, they'd be together the way they both wanted. Her body thrilled to the idea.

"If Peter's mom says it's all right," she said, "then yes, Jesse, you may stay overnight."

Jesse's exuberance bubbled over and the boys high-fived.

Minutes later as Emmy's shift ended, Caroline Wysocki, Peter's mother, enthusiastically agreed to the sleepover. "If you don't mind hot dogs and beans tonight," she said to Jesse. "We're so busy getting our shop ready to open that no one has time to cook."

"I love hot dogs and beans." Jess smacked his lips, and Emmy and Caroline laughed.

"Why don't you come home with us now?" Caroline said.

Jess almost jumped up and down he was so excited.

Emmy nodded. "Okay. I'll pack your overnight bag as soon as I go home, then drop it off. We'd love to reciprocate next weekend."

"Yeah," Jesse said.

Caroline gave her driving directions. Then she, Peter and Jesse left.

Emmy said good-night to Patty and shrugged into her coat. She barely noticed the cold and fog. Before she reached her car, eager to share the good news with Mac, she slid her cell phone from her purse.

Chapter Twelve

The bag of Chinese takeout on the passenger seat smelled good. Mac's mouth watered. Despite his empty stomach, a physically taxing day and the icy fog that forced him to focus carefully on the road, he whistled cheerfully on the drive to Beach Cove Way. His second trip today.

The hours ahead stretched before him, and a fine tension curled in his belly. His muscles felt tighter than a plumb line. A whole night alone with Emmy. Loving her, being loved. God knew, they were both more than ready. This could be his only chance to be with her until morning, and he meant to take full advantage of the situation. Which explained the fistful of condoms in his pocket.

Eager to reach her, he turned onto Beach Cove Way faster than he should have. The road was slicker than it had been an hour ago, and the tires squealed and the van fishtailed.

Heart hammering, Mac gripped the wheel and barely avoided sliding into a tree. "Easy, buddy," he muttered. "You'll get there." He slowed to a crawl.

Since he'd raced home, showered and shaved in record time, Emmy might not even be back yet from dropping off Jesse's overnight bag.

He could hardly wait to make long, slow love with her. Lying down together on a bed. No more fooling around in the Rutherfords' living room, standing up or squeezing into a cramped space on the floor. No more settling for finger sex. Which Mac thoroughly enjoyed, and which provided a release for Emmy. She'd touched him, too, had wanted to stroke him to climax, but he wasn't about to let her. It didn't seem right.

As much as Mac liked pleasuring her that way, he wanted more, needed to join with her the way he needed air to breathe.

He rounded the bend. Emmy's car was parked in her driveway. Soft light shone through cracks in the drapes, beckoning him. His anticipation peaked and his already high spirits soared. Strong feelings swirled in his chest, but he wasn't about to examine them. Or wonder at the tender warmth in Emmy's eyes whenever she looked at him. Tonight was about being together, not analyzing.

He parked where he always did, in front of the Rutherfords'. Just in case. Not that there was much chance of anyone noticing the van. But she worried that Jesse might somehow find out, and you never knew. Why take chances?

Whistling again, his body coiled and thrumming, he exited the van and strode toward the cottage with the takeout and a bottle of wine. The icy air penetrated his shirt, but he wasn't cold. He stepped onto the stoop and knocked.

Almost immediately Emmy opened the door. Jazz music softly floated in the air, rhythmic and suggestive. Perfect.

"Hi." She smiled shyly. Her eyebrows rose a fraction

as she nodded at his Oxford-cloth shirt and slacks. "I've never seen you in anything but a T-shirt and jeans."

"Figured I'd dress up." He combed his gaze over her, noting the way her hair curled prettily around her shoulders and her shift caressed her curves. "Looks as if we're on the same page."

Blushing, she glanced down at herself as if she'd forgotten.

His eyes dropped to her slim, shapely calves. "You look terrific." *And I can't wait to get you naked.* He entered the house and shut the door. "I like that color blue."

"Thanks."

Their eyes held a moment before she gestured at the table, which was set for two. "Hungry?"

As empty as Mac's belly was, at the moment he wanted only to make love with Emmy. "Oh, I'm hungry all right." He set the takeout and wine on the table. "But not for food."

"It's like that for me, too."

The yearning look he knew so well bloomed on her face, and the heat simmering in his veins caught fire. Mac hauled her to him and kissed her, holding nothing back. Showing her with his mouth how badly he wanted her.

With a soft moan, Emmy circled her arms around his neck, her lips as fevered and ravenous as his own, her tongue eager and probing. Mac's body went rock hard.

They stood in the kitchen pressed tightly together, as close as two clothed people could get. They'd been at this point a frustrating number of times before. Still kissing her, Mac cupped her breasts through the soft fabric of her dress. He heard the familiar swift intake of her breath, smelled her woman scent.

His blood roaring, he tore his mouth from hers to nuzzle the sensitive place below her ear. "I want you so much," he murmured against her skin. "Making love to you is all I think about." He nipped gently and felt her quiver. "Day and night."

He slipped his hands under her skirt and grasped her soft behind. And stilled. "You're not wearing panties." Desire raged through him, and he laughed softly. "You vixen."

"That I am." She tipped her head back and gave him a sexy smile that only inflamed him more.

He took her mouth hard and moved his hand between her legs. Gasping, she opened for him. She was already wet and hot.

In the heat clouding his mind, any thought of making slow love together evaporated. His body demanded release. *Now.* A low growl rumbled from his chest. "If we don't head for the bedroom right now, we won't make it."

"There *are* other options." Flushed with need, Emmy glanced over her shoulder at the kitchen counter. A fantasy of his that he'd mentioned once.

"You sure?" he asked.

"Why do you think I spread a bath towel over it?"

Mac required no more encouragement. Pulse pounding in his ears, devouring her mouth, he backed her toward the counter. Lifted her and positioned her on the towel. Slid a condom from his pocket and set it beside her. He helped her unzip and remove the dress. Her lacy, beige bra quickly followed.

He knew her whole body by touch and had gazed at her breasts, but he'd never seen her completely naked. Though he ached to plunge inside her now, he paused to study her. Flushed and soft, her eyes dark with sexual desire, she was perfect.

His.

Reverently he leaned down, molded her firm, heavy breasts in his palms and caressed the sensitive tips with his tongue. Emmy clutched his shoulders, her breathing sweetly ragged. Her nipples swelled and stiffened. Throbbing with need and the desire to pleasure her, Mac continued to nip and lick and suckle until she shifted restlessly.

Eager to give her what she wanted, he mouthed his way down her belly. She tensed when he reached her curls. Widened her thighs and gripped his biceps tightly.

By now he knew what she liked best. He opened her feminine lips. Inserted two fingers inside. Knelt before her and tongued her swollen little bud.

"Oh," she moaned, leaning back until her head bumped the cabinet.

He'd barely begun to taste her before her muscles spasmed around his fingers and she came apart. Mac loved when she let go, loved that he was the one to give her this joy.

When she went silent and still, he pulled back and pushed to his feet. She was pink-cheeked, her lips slightly parted and curled into a satisfied smile. So incredibly beautiful.

As badly as Mac longed to be inside her, if satisfying her in this way was as far as things ever went, it would be enough.

"You're so passionate and responsive," he said, kissing her mouth.

"Thanks to you. You're a very skilled man."

Praise he'd heard from women before. But until this moment, with Emmy smiling at him like he was something special, the words hadn't carried much weight. Humbled, Mac shrugged.

"I can taste myself on your lips," she said.

"Does that bother you?"

She shook her head. "I like it. But let's not focus on me anymore." She glanced at his erection and arched her eyebrows. "It's your turn, Mac. If you don't come inside me soon, I swear I'll die."

"You don't have to ask twice."

In seconds he'd shed his clothes. Emmy had never seen him totally naked. She silently regarded his erection.

"Look what you do to me," he said.

"Oh, I'm looking." She smiled, a vibrant, sexy woman who knew she was in control. "Let me put the condom on you," she said, tearing open the packet.

Mac gritted his teeth against the shock waves of pleasure detonated by her touch. His already hard groin pulsed and swelled even more. "Don't take too long or I'll embarrass myself," he rasped.

"Done. Now love me, Mac, the way we both want." Her eyes fluttered shut and she wrapped her thighs around his waist.

Anchoring her hips in place, Mac thrust deep, until he wasn't sure where he ended and she began.

"Sweet mercy," he groaned. "You feel so damned good."

"I know." His woman swallowed, then made the breathy sound that signaled arousal. "I…I'm going to come again." Her muscles squeezed his penis. "Please, Mac. Move. *Now.*"

He pushed in, pulled back, pushed again. Faster and farther and harder until Emmy cried out. An instant later he followed, the pleasure so great, he saw stars.

When the haze lifted and he returned to the here and now, Emmy was resting against his chest and he was still cradled between her thighs. Awe and tenderness filled him. Because he'd just enjoyed the best sex of his life, he told himself. Anything more was too scary.

"That was worth waiting for." He kissed the crook of her shoulder and felt her shiver. "Fantastic."

"Even better than I dreamed. And I dreamed a *lot.*" She gave Mac a contented smile. "I'm so happy."

Mac hugged her closer. "Yeah, I know."

Her fingers combed through his hair, smoothing it back from his forehead. So incredibly gentle, so soothing. Mac had never felt such peace and contentment. Closing his eyes, he absently stroked the soft skin of her hips and outer thighs.

As she stirred and responded to his touch, he knew that as soon as he recovered he'd make love with her again. Preferably in bed and more slowly. He wanted to share a shower with her, too, and maybe try—

Suddenly Emmy's stomach growled.

"That sounds ominous," he teased, pulling out of her arms.

She looked sheepish. "Guess I'm ready for dinner."

"Me, too. Let's eat that takeout." He handed her his shirt and watched her button it.

The thing was way too big for her, and she rolled the cuffs several times. As loose at it was, when she slid off the counter her nipples poked the cotton.

So damned seductive. Ignoring the fresh need sweeping though him, Mac grabbed his shorts and slacks and turned toward the bathroom. "I'll go clean up."

"And I'll reheat the food."

When he returned to the kitchen, Emmy was at the table, pouring wine. Her hair was tucked neatly behind her ears. She looked cute having dinner in his shirt.

Except that underneath she was naked.

Mac's body tightened and he wanted her even more than before. He could hardly wait to get through the meal and make love with her again.

NOT LONG AFTER the most amazing sex of her life, Emmy dabbed her mouth, then laid her napkin on her empty plate. "That was delicious, Mac. I'm crazy about Chinese food."

"So I noticed." His eyes twinkled. "The way you handled those chopsticks—I'm impressed."

Here she was, sitting across the table from the man she most wanted to be with. Who was more relaxed than she'd ever seen him and gloriously bare-chested. Just the two of them eating and talking as easily as if they dined this way every night. She dreamed of that. Right now she wanted to pinch herself to make sure it was real.

"We ate a ton of Asian food in Oakland, so I've had lots of practice." She nodded at Mac's unused chopsticks. "If you want any pointers…"

"No, thanks, I'll stick with a fork. How about another glass of wine, or seconds of dinner?"

Emmy shook her head. "I've had enough, thanks."

"Not me."

Mac helped himself to more chow mein and fried rice. His biceps flexed. Lord, what an amazing set of muscles. And that chest—broad with a smattering of hair. A flat belly and thick, powerful legs. As for his groin…well, what they said about the size of a man's hands and a certain body part was definitely true. And, oh, the pleasure he gave with his fingers, lips and tongue…

Emmy's body began to hum with the now-familiar need.

Oblivious, Mac devoured his food. Amazed at his

appetite and so in love she felt drunk, Emmy shook her head. She'd never felt this way before, totally full and complete. Certainly not with Chas. He hadn't wanted her love.

Unfortunately neither did Mac. Like Chas, Mac's plans excluded a woman and her son. Having learned her lesson most painfully from Chas, Emmy wasn't going to get in Mac's way. He would never know he owned her heart.

For a moment her world darkened. But she wouldn't ruin this precious time with wishful thinking. Tonight was about here and now, forging cherished memories no one could ever take from her.

Emmy hugged herself. Mac's shirt smelled good—spicy and clean, like him.

Looking up from his now-empty plate, he caught her staring. His brows pulled together. "What?"

She forced a lighthearted shrug. "Just wondering if you'll have room for some of the chocolate cake I pulled from the freezer. There's vanilla ice cream to go with it."

His eyes lit up. "There's always room for dessert. I'll take two scoops with my cake, please."

He started to stack the dishes, but Emmy stopped him.

"Let me clear the table. You sit and finish your wine."

He nodded and sat back.

She rinsed the empty takeout cartons and the plates. As she loaded the dishwasher, Mac made a low, appreciative sound she recognized—a lustful growl that sent her pulse skyrocketing. Slightly breathless, she turned around to find him staring at her through slitted eyes.

"Have I told you how sexy you look in my shirt?"

"Yes." She couldn't help thrusting out her chest,

noting with satisfaction that his eyes darkened. "But feel free to tell me again."

His chair scraped back and he stood. "I changed my mind about what I want for dessert."

"Oh?" Every nerve in her body tensed. "What would you prefer?"

"Let's head for the bedroom and I'll show you."

MAC WOKE UP early, before dawn. Emmy lay beside him, one arm flung across his belly and her face turned into the crook of his shoulder. Her hair smelled faintly of lemons and her tranquil breath fanned his chest, a brush of early-morning sweetness.

Sometime during the night the furnace had turned down, and despite her warmth, the bedroom was cold. With his free hand, Mac tugged the covers over her shoulders.

The bedside lamp glowed softly—he'd wanted to look into her eyes while they made love—and he briefly took in the pale yellow walls and colorful area rug over the beige carpet. Cozy, welcoming colors, a lot like Emmy. Mac smiled and pulled her closer.

She mumbled and nestled into his side, her hand now dangerously close to his groin. His morning erection stood at attention. After what—four times?—he should've had enough, should feel sated. Instead, he wanted her again, more than ever.

Emmy seemed to share his insatiable need to make love. With a wry smile, Mac noted the clothes tossed haphazardly on the floor, a testament to the frenzied passion that only seemed to grow more intense. Oh, eventually they'd managed to make slow, leisurely love. The fourth time. The first three they were too impatient.

She was the most passionate, sexy woman Mac had ever known. He wouldn't mind a repeat tonight and the next night. And the one that followed. Would like to wake up beside her like this every morning.

The thought terrified him.

Uh-uh, he was *not* giving up his dream again. It was his turn to do exactly what he pleased—travel, then go to school full-time. Nothing would stop him. Nothing.

Not even Emmy.

And now he had to get the hell out of Dodge. He slid his arm from under her. "Emmy?"

"Mmm?"

She opened her eyes, stretched and gave him a warm, sleepy smile that made his chest hurt.

Mac cleared his throat. "It's almost five." He swung his legs over the bed and showed her his back. "I should go."

"But I don't have to pick up Jess until ten. Your brothers aren't working today, are they? So you don't have to hurry away. Surely we have time for a leisurely breakfast and—" her voice dropped seductively "—another shower."

If it was anything like last night's…Mac recalled soaping each other all over and the steamy lovemaking they'd enjoyed under the water spray. Passion and pleasure he'd never forget.

Whether he wanted more of that or not—and he did—he wasn't about to shower again or anything else with Emmy.

"Better not." He stood, found his shorts near the bed and pulled them on. Did the same with his slacks. "Don't worry about me. I'll let myself out. Go back to sleep."

She propped herself on her elbow, the blanket barely covering her breasts. A siren, seducing him without even trying.

"Are you working later today?" she asked. "Will you need me to unlock the door?"

Mac enjoyed spending part of his Saturdays on the job, especially when the extra hours put him that much further ahead of schedule. Today he needed to stay away from the Rutherfords' place and Emmy. Until he pulled his crap together.

Busy with his shirt, he shook his head. "I'm only in town two more weeks. There's a lot to do before then. Errands and cleaning out my apartment."

All true. So why did he feel like a lying jerk?

She seemed to buy it, smiling warmly. "Okay."

"I won't call. I don't want Jesse to think something he shouldn't," he added, feeling worse than ever for using her son as an excuse.

"Good idea. So I'll see you Monday morning. Have a good weekend." With a yawn, she sank back down onto the pillow.

"Sleep tight. And thanks for last night."

Mac flipped out the lamp, then padded through the darkness. He found his shoes and socks by the door, where he'd moved them while he and Emmy enjoyed a midnight snack of cake and ice cream after that unforgettable shower.

A few minutes later he was sitting in the van, shivering while he waited for it to warm up. And wondering what in hell he'd been thinking, coming over here last night.

Chapter Thirteen

Monday morning Jesse kissed Emmy's cheek without her asking. "Bye, Mom."

Pleased, she smiled. Saturday morning he'd come home from Peter's tired but happy, and they'd spent a relatively peaceful weekend together.

"I'll see you at the library this afternoon," she said. "Don't forget, it's Groundhog Day."

"Do you think he'll see his shadow?"

"If he does, we'll have six more weeks of winter."

"Ugh." Her son wrinkled his nose.

"Double ugh. As cloudy as it is around here, he probably won't, though." Emmy glanced at her watch. "It's late, Jesse. Hurry!"

"I'm going." He pulled his jacket from the hook. "You'll be glad to see Mac this morning, huh?"

He grinned knowingly, and she suspected that he guessed too much. Well, she never had been good at hiding her feelings.

"He's become a friend," she said. Which was true. If you skipped over the fact that he was also her lover, her very thoughtful, generous and terrific lover, and that she adored him. "And you're right, I *am* looking forward to seeing him."

After the long weekend apart, she could hardly wait. Even if only to say good morning and unlock the Rutherfords' house. If she felt this way today, when Mac left in two weeks she'd surely die. But she wouldn't worry about that now. She intended to enjoy every second of those precious fourteen days, to be with Mac in whatever way possible.

"Be honest, Mom. You like him more than—"

They both heard the bus screech to a stop out front. Jesse rushed out. Thanking her lucky stars for the interruption, Emmy peered out the window. No sign of Mac yet. He must be running late.

Humming, she loaded the dishwasher. She set her lunch beside her purse, then transferred tonight's dinner casserole from the freezer to the refrigerator. The small fern she'd bought and placed on the windowsill over the kitchen sink needed watering, so she took care of that. Next she put on lipstick and checked her hair.

It was nearly eight-thirty now and still no sign of Mac. Where was he? Emmy didn't want to be late for the Monday-morning library meeting.

She was putting her things into the car when at last she heard an engine. Heart lifting, she spun around. Only to see Ian and Brian's black truck approaching. Apparently she wouldn't see Mac this morning, after all.

Swallowing back her disappointment, she headed forward with what she hoped was a friendly smile. "Good morning."

"Hey," Ian said. "Mac's picking up the cabinets. We'll start installing them today, after we hook up the new kitchen sink."

"Sounds exciting." Mac hadn't mentioned that on Saturday, but then, he'd had other things on his mind. She glanced at Brian, noted his dismal expression, and forgot her own low spirits.

"What's the matter, Brian?"

"My girlfriend dumped me." Looking miserable, he kicked at the dirt.

He'd only dated the woman a couple of weeks. He must really like her. "I'm sorry," Emmy said.

"Yeah." He moved ahead of Emmy and Ian to climb the stairs.

Ian shrugged and gave his head a sad shake.

As Emmy reached the top and joined Brian, she touched his arm. "I know how that hurts."

"She wasn't good enough for you, anyway," Ian said.

"That's right." Emmy unlocked the dead bolt.

"Maybe, but I still feel like shi— Like holy heck." Brian glanced at Ian. "No offense, but your great girl-friend and super love life aren't helping."

"Hey, leave Rebecca out of this," Ian said, his eyes soft with affection.

They said goodbye to Emmy and headed inside. She descended the steps and crossed the yard, her mind on their conversation. She so identified with both men, for different reasons.

Ian clearly wanted love and had found it. And so had Emmy. But like Brian, the one she loved didn't return the feeling. Brian's heart was broken, and very soon, hers would be, too.

"IT'S ALMOST five-thirty and past quitting time," Ian said as he helped Mac heft a cabinet. "After we mount this thing, Brian and I are heading to Toddy's for fish and chips and beer. He needs it."

His brother was hurting, and Mac agreed that the local bar at the end of Main Street was a good place for Brian to salve his wounds with greasy food, beer on tap and a game or two of pool. "Good idea," he grunted as he fit the heavy cupboard into place.

Brian, whose face wore the bleak lines of a man with a crushed heart, handed him the drill and screws. "Feel free to join us if you can spare the time. We know you're finishing odds and ends here and running around, getting ready to leave."

Busy securing the cabinet, Mac didn't reply. The drill was too loud. But he thought about the evening ahead. Installing the rest of the cupboards required at least two sets of hands, so that was out. There were a few small jobs he could take care of, like arranging the counter tiles so they'd be easy to grout tomorrow. And his apartment wasn't half cleaned out. Being there for his brother seemed more important than any of that stuff, a good reason to leave shortly.

But Mac wanted to talk to Emmy. After a whole weekend spent kicking himself for staying the night, he hadn't been ready to face her this morning. Still wasn't, but this evening he would, anyway. Things needed to be said.

"Maybe I'll come to Toddy's later," he said after shutting off the drill. "How long will you two be there?"

"Late." Ian eyed him. "But don't worry, no matter how hungover Brian is tomorrow, I'll get him here on time."

"I know that." Mac clapped Brian's sagging shoulder. "Hang in there, little bro. This, too, shall pass."

With a grudging nod, Brian shrugged into his jacket. Behind his back Ian exchanged glances with Mac. They both knew that in time their brother would rebound.

Once they left, Mac sweated over what to say to Emmy. That from now on, every minute of his life was crammed with last-minute details to see to before he left town. That as busy as he was, he couldn't be with her anymore, not the way he wanted. No more sticking around for kisses, no more making love, no more *anything* outside casual conversation. That sounded good.

As soon as her car pulled into her driveway he flipped off all the house lights except for the table lamp in the living room. He turned on the porch light and stepped outside.

Though he was hidden by the fir trees, the sound of the Rutherfords' door closing caught Emmy's and Jesse's attention. Both turned toward him. Mac stepped out of the shadows and waved. Jesse waved back, but instead of bounding over, took his mother's things to their front door, unlocked it and disappeared inside. Fine with Mac. What he wanted to say wasn't for the boy's ears.

Emmy headed toward Mac, her gait purposeful but graceful. Even in the dim streetlamp, he saw her warm, radiant smile. So special and beautiful…

His chest expanded and his resolve wavered, but only for a moment. Steeling his heart, he nodded unsmilingly. "Hey."

"Hi." She hurried up the steps. Breathless, she crossed the deck. "I missed you this morning. Did you pick up the cabinets? I'd love to see them." In a low voice she added, "I asked Jesse to put the casserole in the oven, so I can't stay long. Later, when he showers—"

"I won't be here then. Brian's hurting and I'm meeting him and Ian at Toddy's."

"I heard about that. That's sweet of you."

At the moment Mac felt anything but sweet. "It's

what brothers do for each other." He cleared his throat, rocked back on his heels. "Listen, Emmy, we both know I'm leaving soon and—"

"We still have two whole weeks."

"And I'll be swamped every minute, tying up loose ends and getting ready."

She blinked at him. "We're all busy, Mac. Don't use the trip as an excuse. At least have the decency to be honest with me."

The confused, hurt look on her face ate at him. Mac rubbed the space between his eyes. "Being with you…it's dangerous. You're starting to care." Never mind his own feelings.

"Of course I care." Her eyes flashed and her chin jutted out. "After what we shared the past few weeks, how could I not?"

The need to reach out and ease that high, defensive chin back down was overwhelming. Mac clasped his hands behind him and leaned against the unforgiving siding.

Understanding dawned on her face. "You're scared."

"The hell I am. Why would I be?"

"That's a good question. I know how you feel about responsibility, Mac, and I don't expect anything from you. You've made it clear often enough. You're not interested in a relationship with a woman who has a son."

"Mom?"

Jesse stood on the bottom step, looking as if he'd been sucker punched.

Emmy jerked toward him, her forced smile fooling no one. "Hi, honey. You're so quiet I didn't know you were here."

Neither had Mac. He'd been too engrossed in Emmy. She shot him a quick, anxious look and he knew she wondered how much of their conversation her son had caught. Mac shared her concern.

He nodded. "Hey, Jess."

The boy narrowed his eyes. Hostility radiated from him. If looks could kill... He'd overheard something, all right.

"I couldn't remember whether you wanted the oven turned to 350 or 375," Jesse mumbled. "Guess I should've just picked one."

"I don't know what you're thinking," Mac said, "but our discussion has nothing to do with you."

"Right." Sarcasm dripped from the word. Jesse pinned his attention on Emmy. "Which temperature, Mom?"

"Three fifty."

"'Kay." The boy pivoted and hurried toward the cottage.

"I'll be there as soon as I lock the door," Emmy called after him. She bit her lip and pulled her arms close to her body. "Look what just happened. This is why I don't date or get involved."

"For what it's worth I'm sorry about Jesse." But Mac wasn't sorry about the rest. Loving Emmy—he'd never forget that.

She didn't seem to hear him. "It's okay that you don't want to be with me again, because I need to spend my time with Jesse. *He* is my priority." A haunted look crossed her face. "I don't know how I could've forgotten something so important."

"Don't beat yourself up, Emmy. Any fool with eyes knows he comes first with you. You care so much about him and his feelings that no matter what he heard just now, he has no idea what happened between us." Mac started to reach for her, then dropped his arms. "Believe me, you're as good a mother as you always have been."

"Am I?"

Her eyes were filled with doubt and uncertainty, the same troubled expression she'd worn right before he'd kissed her the first time and started down the path that had led them here.

Turning away, she bolted the door, then pocketed the key. "I'm going home now to straighten things out." She nodded coolly, her distance chilling his very marrow. "Good night."

Walking away from him with her gaze on the ground and her shoulders hunched, she looked as bereft as he felt.

IN ONE HELL of an ugly mood, bowed against the heavy mist and freezing rain, hands deep in the pockets of his denim jacket, Mac trudged toward Toddy's. His well-meaning talk with Emmy had gone from bad to miserable, and not only because Jesse had overheard God knew what of their conversation. Emmy's horrified response to Jesse's reaction, her self-blame and guilty expression were indelibly etched in Mac's mind.

At least she agreed with him, that what they shared was over and done with. A good thing, right? Except that his heart felt bruised and sore.

Main Street was only a few blocks from the water, and tonight the smell of the sea clung to every building and tree. With weather like this, there was sure to be a halo-shaped cloud hovering over the ocean. A fascinating phenomenon that had entertained Mac and his brothers many times. On any other evening he'd have wandered down to the beach to check it out. Tonight he wanted only to hang with Ian and Brian, share a pitcher and play pool.

He pushed through the scarred wood door. The usual

odors of beer and stale cigarettes tickled his nostrils. A recent law banned smoking in here, and the owner had since painted the place and added a few fichus trees and ferns. But nothing could wash away the decades of smoke that had permeated every surface or change the fact that people came to Toddy's to forget their problems through drink.

Being a Monday night in the middle of winter, the place was mostly empty. Four of the bar stools stood vacant and only a few booths were taken. An old Jane's Addiction song pounded from the jukebox, the raucous rock music suiting Mac's mood just fine.

He looked around for Ian and Brian, but didn't see them. Probably in the back room, shooting pool. He'd check. First, though, he'd order a burger and a beer.

He was on his way to the bar when he spotted them in a corner booth with a near-empty pitcher. Heads bent toward the table and deep in conversation, neither saw him. As he drew closer he almost tripped over his bootlace. He stooped down to tie it. The music stopped, and suddenly it was easy to hear them.

"I'm gonna hate it when Mac leaves," Ian said.

Mac smiled. That was real nice.

"Yeah," Brian said. "But I'll hate running the company more."

"Amen, and I'll drink to that."

Shocked, Mac froze.

"I'm feeling so crappy right now," Brian went on, "that I'm thinking about taking Emmy's advice and telling him how I really feel."

"Are you kidding?" Ian said. "After everything he did for us? No way. We're doing this, period. Mac's counting on us, and we owe him. It's only three years."

"Don't you think I know that?" Brian said. "But three years is a long time. Every day it's harder to pretend that I like the remodeling business. And now Bethany's dumped me… It was almost frickin' impossible today. The only reason *you're* handling it so well is because you're in love, and that makes anything bearable. I need a lot more to drink. Let's split what's left in the pitcher."

"Pour it, bro. You're right. Before Rebecca, fighting the urge to bail every day was much harder."

There was a pause, and Mac knew his brothers were sipping beer.

"There's still time to apply for the PhD program at the universities I checked out," Brian said. "I'm tempted to do it."

"Not for three years, you won't."

"Okay, okay, you win," Brian muttered. "I'll stay."

"That's the spirit. We need a new pitcher, and it's my round. I wonder if Mac will ever show up."

Hoping they wouldn't see him, Mac crouched lower.

Brian snorted. "Would *you* be here if you could fool around with Emmy, instead?"

"No way. Emmy's hot—for an older woman."

Mac frowned. And not just because his brother shared his opinion. He and Emmy had been so careful. How in hell did Brian and Ian know what they'd been doing? Unless she'd told them. They'd certainly confided in her. This bugged him a lot. His brothers should've come to him, not Emmy. That she knew how they felt about running his company but hadn't bothered to enlighten him also rankled. He felt like a damned fool.

"While you get the beer I'll be in the men's room," Brian said.

Mac waited until they both ambled off before he

straightened. With no idea what to do and his mind spinning, he quickly left the tavern.

Once outside he headed for the beach. The sleet had stopped, but the wind had picked up, and there was no one else on the street. Buffeted by the strong gust, Mac tromped down the rest of the block, rounded the corner and strode down the gently sloping hill that led to the beach. He passed the group of huts where artists sold their wares during tourist season. Now they were shuttered and dark.

Planting his feet in the sand a few yards from the sea, he stared out. With the moon obscured by clouds and the nearest streetlight a block away, he couldn't see anything, much less the halo. It was there, though, he knew it.

The wind whipped his face. Waves crashed and retreated. The cold, damp sea air penetrated Mac's jacket and clothes.

But the real chill came from inside him.

For so many reasons. His brothers didn't want to run the business he loved, had only agreed out of obligation. Without so much as discussing the matter with him. The amazing connection Mac had shared with Emmy was forever broken. And Jesse? Mac had no idea what the boy thought, but it couldn't be good.

What a mess.

Teeth chattering, he turned away from the water and plodded toward the street. His plans—his whole life—seemed to be unraveling, and he didn't know how to stop it.

Chapter Fourteen

It was after eleven and Jesse was supposed to be asleep. He'd been about to drop off when his mom peeked in to check on him. Now he lay in the dark, thinking about what she'd repeated several times tonight.

"There never was anything between Mac and me. How could there be? He's leaving soon."

Jesse knew differently. He'd seen his mom after she locked up at the Rutherfords'. Glowing like she'd swallowed the porch light, with her eyes all soft and dreamy.

He knew what that meant. She had feelings for Mac, maybe even loved him. The warm way Mac looked at her meant that he cared, too. And the…

His thoughts dissolved as a muffled sound he hadn't heard since kindergarten floated from his mom's bedroom. Sobs, probably cried into her pillow so he wouldn't hear.

The same, secret way she'd cried after his father had left. Jesse's heart seized up, and for a few seconds he couldn't breathe. His mother's pain hurt that much. And it was all his fault. Just like before.

"You don't want a woman with a son," she'd said to Mac.

By the look on Mac's face Jesse saw that she'd spoken the truth. That Mac liked his mom, but didn't want Jesse. That was the real reason he was still leaving town.

Wishing he had the teddy bear he'd thrown away years ago, Jesse curled into a tight ball and squeezed his eyes shut. He'd tried so hard to be good, but it was never enough. He was... What was that word he'd learned in school last week? *Defective.*

No wonder Mac didn't care about him.

Knowing he'd ruined his mom's chance of happiness was almost unbearable. Pain cut like a knife slash. And Tyrell had explained how much that hurt.

Lying miserable and alone, Jesse pictured tall, skinny Tyrell, whom he hadn't missed or thought of in weeks. Tyrell didn't care that Jesse was defective. He still liked him. Had invited him into the Street Kings. To cheer himself up Jesse made the secret sign Tyrell had shown him when he'd pressed Jesse to join the gang, a hand gesture only other members knew. In a strange sort of way, circling his fingers together helped and he felt better now. He also came to a decision.

His mom had suffered enough. She deserved her chance at happiness.

"This time, you'll get it," he quietly stated. He'd make sure of that.

He didn't want to leave the island because he liked living here. But if he went, Mac would stay. Jesse knew it. He'd pack a few things, whatever fit under the books in his backpack. Go to school to avoid a call from the principal, but instead of taking the bus to the library, he'd cut out at the end of the day. Walk to Halo Island Bank and empty the savings account his mom had opened for him. He'd been saving for an Xbox for a while now, and had put away almost a hundred dollars. From there it wasn't far to the ferry terminal and a boat to Anacortes. He'd call Tyrell to let him know he was coming. Then he'd hitchhike to Oakland.

He'd never hitchhiked before, but Tyrell had. It wasn't hard. You just had to smile and stick out your thumb. He'd never taken money out of his savings, either. A hundred bucks seemed like a lot, but how many times had his mom complained that stretching a dollar wasn't easy? Jesse worried he wouldn't have enough. He knew where she kept her rainy-day money—in an empty frozen-vegetable box in the freezer. The thought of taking it made him feel sick, but he had no choice.

Tears rolled down his cheeks. Just like his mom, he covered his face with a pillow and cried.

TUESDAY MORNING Emmy left for work without waiting for Mac. She simply scribbled a note, stuck it under the mat with the corner showing and unlocked the door. She didn't know yet what she'd do tonight. Maybe she'd lock up after he left.

She had her pride, she told herself as she turned from Beach Cove Way onto Treeline Road, and had learned her lesson. The man didn't want to spend even a fraction of his last weeks with her. Fine. She'd survived the breakup of her marriage, and she would survive this.

Ahead of her, a car pulled out of a small road not unlike Beach Cove Way. To avoid hitting it, Emmy braked. The tires squealed. Unless she wanted to get involved in an accident, she'd better pay attention to her driving. Yet even as she scolded herself to keep her mind on the road, her thoughts moved to Jesse and her own sorry neglect of him. Thanks to a selfish preoccupation with Mac, she'd all but ignored Jesse's needs, putting him second. Well, she was paying for that now.

Since overhearing part of her conversation with Mac, her son had morphed back into his argumentative, defensive self. Which scared Emmy. She replayed breakfast this morning. Aware that her eyes were red from crying and not wanting Jess to know, she'd used eyedrops and applied concealer to the dark circles underneath before her son's alarm went off.

"Good morning, sleepyhead," she said when he entered the kitchen, trying her best to pretend that nothing was different.

But she knew right away that over the past thirteen hours, everything had changed. If Jesse's grunted reply and closed, hostile expression hadn't alerted her, his too-baggy jeans and Street Kings T-shirt did. It had been so long since he'd worn those clothes she was sure he'd put them away forever.

Scared, she'd tried again. "What can I fix you for breakfast?"

"Nothin'."

The old tension between them felt as heavy and uncomfortable as it used to be. Or was that her imagination? Battling despair, she tried again, smiling. "Are you sure? There's time to fix pancakes or—"

"I don't want you to make me anything! I can take care of myself."

He found a bowl and a box of cereal and banged the cabinets shut, anger radiating from his jerky motions. Anger no amount of coaxing or willingness to talk had appeased. Emmy had even brought up yesterday afternoon, though Lord knew, last night she'd talked the subject to death.

"If you're upset about Mac, don't be. I—"

"I'm not, so get off my case!"

Shocked by the rage in his voice, she shut her mouth, and for the rest of breakfast, remained silent. When Jesse left, she barely rated a goodbye, let alone a kiss. At least he'd remembered to grab his jacket without a reminder. That was something, she supposed. She knew she'd have to work extra hard to bring back her son's smile. If she could just figure out how.

Raising a boy alone seemed a never-ending challenge. With a sigh she signaled, then pulled into the library parking lot. She was early, but not as early as Sally, whose car was already in its usual slot. While Emmy drove into the adjacent space she wished she could relive the evening. She imagined walking with Jesse into the cottage and not talking with Mac until her son had stepped into the shower. Then he wouldn't have heard what he shouldn't have.

But there was no going back, and nothing ever came from wishing for what might have been.

As she unbuckled her seat belt and reached for her purse and lunch on the passenger seat, her cell phone rang. Thinking it might be Mac, that he'd missed her note and hadn't tried the door, she reached for it with an anticipation she no longer wanted and certainly couldn't afford. The display said, "Melinda Rutherford."

"Hi, Emmy. Is this a bad time to call?"

"Not at all. I just got to the library, but I'm a few minutes early. How's your uncle?"

"Much better, thanks. Good news. We'll be home tomorrow, around dinnertime. Will you let Mac know?"

"Certainly." Emmy was relieved that after today she

wouldn't have to leave him notes or wait around for him. She also felt wretched. "This is great timing, as your kitchen is almost done."

"That's Mac, finishing on schedule. We can't wait to see our beautiful new space. What do you think of it?"

That Mac was very skilled with his hands, hands that would never again touch her. "I haven't been inside since Friday," she said. "But I'm told that most of the cabinets are in."

"I'm so excited! See you soon." Melinda hung up.

Determined to bury her heavy heart and make the most of the day, Emmy squared her shoulders as she crossed the parking lot. When she pushed through the library door she pasted a happy expression on her face.

STAYING UPBEAT was easier said than done, especially with few patrons in the library to distract her. By midmorning, while standing at the portable book cart, organizing volumes to reshelve, Emmy lost the battle. Shoulders sagging, she morosely returned a biography to its slot.

Sally, who sat nearby working at her desk, frowned. "You look so melancholy. Did you get bad news today?"

"Not exactly." Emmy pulled absently on her hair. "I'm having problems with Jesse again." Sally, Mason and Patty all knew about her son's reluctance to adjust to life on the island.

"He seemed all right on Friday. What happened?"

The older woman looked genuinely concerned, in a way Emmy's mom had never been. Badly in need of a friendly ear and some motherly advice, Emmy bit her lip. "It's a long story."

"And it's a quiet morning. I have time. Pull up a chair and sit."

Emmy did. She told Sally about Chas and how Jesse had changed after he'd walked out. About Tyrell Barker and the Street Kings, and how in the past few weeks, Jess had rarely mentioned the gang or Oakland. She explained about Mac, that she'd foolishly fallen in love. She finished with the conversation Jesse had overheard yesterday and how his dark mood had returned. She shared everything except that she and Mac had spent a passionate night together. That was too private.

"Falling in love with an unavailable man was the wrong thing for me and my son," she finished, "but there it is. This morning I'm nursing a broken heart. I'm also worried sick about Jesse." She tried to smile. "Aren't you glad you asked?"

"That's a lot on your plate," Sally said with a sympathetic smile. "I completely understand about Mac. As you already know, I think he's pretty special. Even if you didn't mean to fall for him, you and I both know that it's impossible to control feelings."

"That's no excuse for ignoring Jesse. He deserves my full attention."

"I'm not sure he does." Sally frowned. "He's at the age where boys start to stretch their wings and grow up. I've raised two sons, so I speak from experience."

While Emmy mulled that over, Sally continued.

"I know how much you love Jesse, but who says his needs are more important than yours? They're not."

Emmy wondered over this. "That's something I never considered."

"You should. Kids are smart. If you don't take care of your own wants and aren't happy, no matter how much attention you give Jesse, he won't be, either."

Emmy thought about her own childhood and her emotionally distant mother. With startling clarity she realized she'd been so afraid of shutting out Jesse the same way, she'd overcompensated by smothering him with warmth and concern. *Smother* being the operative word.

"Wow." She sat back and shook her head. "Has anyone ever told you that you'd make a top-notch therapist?"

Without an ounce of self-consciousness, Sally nodded. "Several people, including my husband. But books are my great love, and I prefer running the library. Something else just came to mind. Jesse no doubt senses your sadness over Mac. His dark mood could be a reflection of that."

Certain that her son knew nothing of her broken heart, Emmy shook her head. "I'm positive he doesn't. We talked a lot about Mac and me last night. I explained that with Mac leaving town, we could never be more than friends. I've been very careful to hide my deeper feelings from him."

"He probably knows more than you realize. You might think about openly sharing your pain with him."

While Emmy considered the suggestion, the door opened. A group from the Senior Citizens' Center across town wandered in, and the conversation ended.

AFTER A NIGHT spent wrestling with decisions, Mac navigated the fog en route to the Rutherfords', knowing exactly what he had to do. He was going to have it out with Brian and Ian, then fire their sorry behinds.

But since he still needed their help today, he'd wait until this evening. The rest of the project—laying the counter tile, taking care of the trim and whatever else was left—he could do by himself. And by God, he *would* finish this job on time, even if that meant working twenty hours a day.

He also wanted to ask Emmy a few questions. Such as why she didn't tell him about Ian and Brian. That she'd kept their secret from him stung. Aside from that, he wondered how she was doing. Jesse, too.

Mac hoped she'd stopped beating herself up over her son. Knowing Emmy, she hadn't. As he rounded the bend, he glanced far too eagerly toward her cottage. To his surprise, the place was dark. Her car was gone, too. His disappointment, as sharp as the new blade of his circular saw, surprised him. Because he needed answers, he told himself. And he still hoped they could be friends.

After the way things had ended yesterday? Yeah, right. With a self-derisive snort, Mac parked in his usual spot.

Figuring she'd unlocked the Rutherfords' door, he trudged up the steps. He spotted the folded note under the mat. Opened it to find one terse, impersonal line: *The door's unlocked.*

To this house. Not Emmy's. He had no doubt that from now on, her door was closed to him. Glum, he wiped his feet and stepped inside.

AS THE DAY progressed and Emmy mulled over Sally's advice, she decided the woman was right. Jesse deserved the truth. Yes, she cared deeply for Mac and, yes, she was hurt that he didn't feel the same way, but that in time she'd get over him. Hopefully her frankness would encourage Jess to be equally open, the start of a better relationship.

Now that she'd made up her mind, she could hardly wait to see her son. When Mason pushed through the library door just before the beginning of his three-o'clock shift, she knew it wouldn't be long before the school bus stopped down the block.

Mason shook out his umbrella. "It's miserable out there," he said.

The door opened again and a fortysomething redhead with apple cheeks and a windblown bun blew in. "Phew," she said, laughing.

Emmy knew at once that this was Connie O'Connor, local storyteller and today's after-school program guest. Sally and Mason, who knew the woman, called out greetings. Then Mason took his and Connie's coats to the staff room.

"We spoke on the phone." With a smile Emmy stood, rounded the desk and welcomed the visitor. "I'm Emmy Logan."

"Ah, yes, Halo Island's newest librarian." Connie returned the friendly expression and shook Emmy's hand with a cold but firm hand. "Welcome to town. It's nice to meet you."

Emmy offered her a beverage. The storyteller wanted chamomile tea, and Sally went off to brew herself a mug, too.

"The kids will get here soon," Emmy said. "Let me show you where we'll be this afternoon." She ushered Connie into the meeting room.

"Could we push the chairs and tables aside?" Connie asked. "That way everyone can sprawl on the floor."

"That sounds fun." Emmy imagined sitting near Jesse—not too close, but close enough to watch his face while he enjoyed the story—and smiled to herself.

Just as they finished clearing a space, Mason peeked in. "The munchkins have arrived."

Ready to greet everyone, especially Jesse, Emmy

waited by the meeting-room door. Kids filed in. As always she spoke to each one, with Connie joining in. No sign of Jess or Peter yet, but they were often last. She finally spotted Peter, but oddly, Jesse wasn't with him.

"Where's Jess?" she asked, wondering if her son had deliberately dragged his feet to be late, as he had those first few times.

Peter shrugged. "I don't know, Ms. Logan. I haven't seen him since lunch. He said he wasn't coming today."

Emmy widened her eyes. "He wasn't on the bus?"

Peter shook his head.

"Maybe Mrs. Hatcher asked him to stay after school for some reason," Emmy said.

But wouldn't Jesse have called to let her know? Then again, he'd been so angry this morning he just might *want* her to worry. That was probably it, Emmy assured herself. Yet the first shards of alarm pierced her stomach. She hunkered down in front of Peter and peered at him. "I want you to think carefully, Peter. Did Jesse say anything to you about where he planned to go this afternoon?"

The boy bit his lip. "He wasn't supposed to skip the after-school program, was he?"

Emmy shook her head. Peter paled, his face pinched in worry, and she realized her teeth were clenched. She forced a friendlier expression. "It's okay, Peter. You didn't do anything wrong."

She patted his shoulder, then straightened and moved to Connie's side. "My son is missing," she said in a low voice. "I need to figure out where he is. Would you mind introducing yourself, or should I call Mason?"

The storyteller's eyes darkened with concern. "Don't worry about me, I can do it. Just go find your boy."

"I'll bet he's feeling bad about this morning," Sally said when Emmy told her. "He probably went home."

"He doesn't have a key to the house." And it was cold and rainy outside. He could be at the Rutherfords', but after yesterday, Emmy doubted that. "I think I'll call the school."

"Jesse was unusually quiet today," Liza Hatcher said. "I asked him if he felt sick, but he assured me he was fine. I can't imagine where'd he'd be. Unless... The students have an assignment due on Friday, so he might be in the school library. Hold on and I'll put you through."

Jess wasn't there, and after what seemed an interminably long time as Emmy was routed to various areas in the school with no one able to locate him, she grew increasingly worried. Finally there was nothing to do but hang up. Mason and Sally, who stood waiting across her desk, looked as anxious and upset as she felt.

"Well?" Mason asked.

Emmy clasped her hands together, barely registering how clammy they were. "No one at school has seen Jesse or knows where he is."

"Don't you think you ought to check with Mac?" Sally said.

A call couldn't hurt. Mac's cell phone rang eight times before clicking to voice mail. Without leaving a message, Emmy disconnected. "He doesn't answer."

"Go home," Sally said. "And please let us know when you find Jesse."

Chapter Fifteen

As the day wore on and Mac's bad mood festered, he reined in his temper by sheer force of will. And continued to be amazed by his kid brothers. Yeah, Brian was down about Rebecca, but just like Ian, he ribbed and goaded his twin and Mac. They worked as hard as always. Mac wondered why neither of them wanted an acting career. They were pros.

Now that he knew how they really felt about remodeling he saw what they hid so well. The forced heartiness, the long faces when they thought he wasn't looking. Brian still reading those dry-looking communication books should've been a dead giveaway. Mac gave his head a mental shake. How could he have been so frigging obliv—

"Yo, Mac," Brian said. "I repeat, hand me those wooden caps so I can cover the screw heads on these cabinets."

Too ticked off to reply, Mac scowled and tossed over the caps. He glanced at his watch. Almost three-thirty. The ninety minutes left before he could air his thoughts seemed an eternity.

"You're still sore that Emmy didn't wait around to let you in this morning, aren't you?" Ian said.

In no mood to discuss his love life—or lack thereof—Mac clamped his jaw shut.

Brian grinned. "You'll see her this afternoon. Then you two can—"

Enough was enough. "Knock it off. I don't know how you found out about Emmy and me, but it doesn't matter. We're through." He gave Ian a deadpan look. "But I'm with you, Ian, she's hot. For an older woman."

Brian looked taken aback. "Say again?"

"What are you talking about?" Ian tugged his goatee.

More b.s. Mac snapped. "I didn't bring you two up to be liars. Bad enough that you do it at all. But lying to me… I'm mad as hell at you both."

Ian blanched. Looking like a thief who'd just been caught, Brian froze.

Reactions that would've been funny, except that Mac's future, his *life*, was on the line. "Your dirty secret's out," he said. "I know you hate working in the business."

His brothers traded uneasy glances, then Brian sighed. "Emmy told you, didn't she?"

"Nope. You did. I was in Toddy's last night and heard the words straight from your two-sided mouths."

"But we never saw you," Brian said.

Mac's cell phone rang. Ignoring it, he crossed his arms. "That's not my problem and not the issue."

"Aren't you going to answer that?" Ian said. "Might be important."

"So's this. Whoever it is can leave a message."

"You've been holding all this in since last night?" Ian frowned. "How come you haven't said anything till now?"

"I needed time to think. Why'd you bullshit me?"

"What you heard was just harmless bitching," Brian said. "We're committed to putting in our three years."

Ian nodded. "We want to do it, Mac. We owe you."

"Yeah, well, I've changed my mind. I don't want either of you working in my company just to do me a favor."

"But, Mac—"

He silenced Brian with a stern look. "The heavy work here is done. I'll finish the rest myself. I want you two to go after the careers *you* want."

"But we owe you," Ian repeated.

That they thought so was Mac's fault, and he regretted raising them to believe it. "You want to pay me back?" he asked. "Be happy, productive citizens. And don't ever lie to me again."

He didn't hide his anger or his disappointment. In the silence that fell, he could almost see the wheels grind in their brains as they digested this turn of events.

"What do you really want to do?" Mac looked from Brian to Ian. "And don't either of you try to con me."

His brothers exchanged a glance. After a brief silence, Ian spoke. "All I ever wanted was a job as a computer programmer."

Which made sense. Mac nodded. From his brothers' conversation last night he already knew Brian's ambition. He asked, anyway. "Brian?"

"I'd like to get a PhD in communications, then teach or maybe consult with companies needing help with various media."

Mac nodded again. "Do it. Both of you. With my blessing."

"You sure about this?" Ian asked.

"I said I was."

"What'll you do without us?" Brian asked. "You're leaving in less than two weeks. You don't have time to find anyone else to run the business."

As Mac well knew. With no one to take over he'd have to close up shop. The words stuck in his throat, too painful to say.

"You can't just shut down," Ian said. "This company means too much to you."

So true. Mac had worked long and hard to build his business. He loved what he did. The company was a big part of him, and the thought of starting over in three years made him feel cold inside.

Hips canted against the counter, he stuffed his hands in his pockets and stared at his scuffed boots. And thought about canceling his travel plans and forgetting about heading off to college. But that felt just as bad.

"We've already lined up three more jobs from now through spring," Brian pointed out. "And there are four other people waiting for slots this summer. We can't just leave them high and dry."

Mac wasn't sure what to do about that. Suddenly rapid footsteps pounded across the porch. Emmy burst through the door, wild-eyed and pale.

"I tried to call you, but you didn't answer," she said to Mac. "Is Jesse here?"

Wishing he'd answered his cell and wondering what was wrong, Mac shook his head. "Haven't seen him." Didn't expect to, either. He was pretty sure the kid hated him for hurting his mother. "Shouldn't he be at the library with you?"

"He didn't show up. He's not at school, either. No one knows where he is." Emmy closed her eyes and shuddered. "I think he ran away."

"WE'LL FAN OUT," Mac told his brothers. "Ian, you and Brian cover Main Street, the beach and anyplace else you think Jess might be. I'll scout out the ferry terminal."

"The ferry terminal?" Emmy echoed weakly.

"That's the only way off the island. Unless you catch an Island Air seaplane, and I doubt Jess can afford that. Does he have any money?"

"I don't know," Emmy said. "He gets an allowance every week, but he puts most of that into the bank." She bit her lip. "He might have enough for a ticket."

Mac glanced at his brothers. "Either of you know when the next boat leaves for Anacortes?"

"Not exactly, but when we went to Seattle a few weeks ago, there were only two runs out and back—one in the morning and one in the afternoon," Ian said as he whipped out his iPhone. "Hold on while I call up the winter schedule."

While they waited tensely for the site to load, Emmy fidgeted. "What if we're too late? What if Jess is already gone?"

"Unless he caught the ten-ten this morning, there's still time," Ian said, studying the little screen. "The next boat leaves in twenty minutes."

"His friend Peter saw him at lunch today. That leaves out the morning ferry. Oh, God, Mac. What if he boarded the afternoon boat?"

"Only takes ten minutes to drive to the terminal," Mac said. "I'll head over right now."

"I'll come with you," Emmy said.

He shook his head. "You stay home in case Jesse shows up there."

"I can't just wait around and do nothing. I'll go crazy." She wrung her hands and rocked on her feet.

Time was of the essence and Mac had to go. But Emmy needed reassuring. More than that, as close as she was to the edge of hysteria, it was essential she did *some-thing*. "Why don't you notify the police," he suggested.

Since Jess had only been missing for a few hours, they probably wouldn't do anything, but she'd feel better making the call. Mac cupped her shoulders and realized she was trembling with fear. "Jesse's okay, Emmy. Stay calm and stay strong."

"That's not so easy." Her eyes filled. "All right."

"That's my girl." Not caring that his brothers were watching, Mac tucked her hair behind her ears, then stroked his thumbs over her soft cheeks. "If any of us finds out anything, we'll call right away. You do the same."

With that, he and his brothers headed out.

At four-fifteen, the heavily clouded sky was almost dark. Keeping an eye out for traffic cops, Mac floored the van. And thought about Jesse. When he found that kid—and he meant to—he'd give him a piece of his mind, and it wouldn't be pretty. Scaring his mom like this. Scaring *him*.

If anything happened to Jesse… Mac quaked at the very thought. And realized he cared about the boy. A lot. Damned kid had worked his way under Mac's skin. Just as his mother had. Well, not quite like that.

For a man not wanting to get involved, he sure was tangled up. Snickering and shaking his head in amazement, Mac passed a truck lumbering way too slowly. Between Emmy and Jesse and this mess with his brothers, he hadn't a clue where his life was headed. But it wasn't anywhere near the direction he'd aimed for.

Traveling and going full-time to college. Big dreams he'd held on to for so long now. Did he really still want them?

His cell phone rang. It was Emmy. To free his hands, he put her on speaker. "What's up?"

"The bank just called. Jesse was there half an hour ago trying to close out his savings account."

"Did they let him?"

"No, thank goodness. Since he's a minor they need my signature for that."

"Why'd they wait so damned long to contact you?"

"I don't know. I just thought of something. Hang on, while I put the phone down."

The stoplight ahead turned yellow. Gunning the engine, Mac sped through the intersection.

Emmy came back on the line, her voice shaking. "Jesse took my rainy-day money, Mac."

"How much are we talking about?"

"Almost three hundred dollars."

She sounded utterly bleak. Mac wished he was there to hold and comfort her. He wished a lot of things. But right now, he needed to get to the ferry terminal and stop Jesse. *Let the kid be there. Please.*

"Call Ian and Brian and let them know, will you?" he said. "And hang tight, Emmy. We'll find him."

MAC WAS A SCANT half mile from the ferry terminal when his high beams illuminated a small figure walking on the side of the road, his hoody bowed against the rain and his thumb out. By the baggy jeans and trudging gait, he knew he'd located Jesse.

Relieved and also spitting-nails mad, Mac checked that there was no traffic behind him, hit the brakes and screeched to a halt beside the boy.

Jesse's head whipped around. His eyes widened in shock.

Leaning sideways, Mac opened the passenger door. "Get in."

The boy glanced toward the dark woods behind him, and Mac feared he'd bolt. "Don't make me ask twice," he warned in the voice he'd used on his brothers back in high school when they balked.

It had worked then and did now. Expression carefully blank, Jesse tossed his backpack onto the floor and climbed into the van. His stiff back and set expression screamed belligerence and contempt. He smelled like a wet dog.

"Buckle up."

Jesse's fingers groped clumsily for the seat belt while shivers shook him. Kid must be frozen. Mac turned up the heat, then aimed the vents at the passenger seat.

He drove a hundred yards to a wide turnaround and pulled into it. He hauled on the brake and set the flashers to alert other drivers. "Your mother's worried sick," he said, handing over his cell phone. "Call her."

Now the boy looked scared. "Do I have to?"

"Yep."

As rain pummeled the car, Jess dialed. "Mom? It's me, Jesse." He glanced at Mac, his face dark. "Yeah, I'm with Mac." He listened. "Yes, near the ferry. I'm fine." More silence. "Please, don't cry, Mom." His face screwed up as if he was fighting his own tears.

"Give me the phone," Mac said, his gruffness hiding his own tumultuous feelings. Before speaking to Emmy, he sucked in a deep breath and gentled his voice. "Your son is wet and cold, but he's fine. Let my brothers and the police know, okay?"

"Police?" Jesse squeaked in fear.

Holding the phone to his ear, Mac gave the boy a grave nod. "Jesse and I are going to have a little talk. Then I'll bring him home."

Mac switched on the interior lights. He swiveled in his seat to face Jesse. "Confession time. Why'd you do it?"

The boy stared at his lap. "She's better off without me."

Mac wanted to shake some sense into that foolish eleven-year-old brain, but that wouldn't help matters. "You really think that?" He snorted. "You're the center of her life. Without you she'd..." His voice broke with feeling. "She'd never be happy again."

"I don't believe you."

Now Jess was looking at him, his teeth squeezing his lip and his face a mask of pain and guilt. Something was bothering him.

"What's going through your head?" Mac asked.

"You'd never understand."

"Try me."

Looking indecisive, Jesse again dropped his gaze. Following a gut instinct, Mac waited without speaking, giving the boy the time he needed. His patience paid off. After a few long moments Jesse raised his head and broke the silence.

"My mom...she's never had a boyfriend. I don't think she wanted one before, but then she met you." His hands fidgeted on his knees and the words rushed out. "She really likes you, Mac, maybe even loves you. But you don't want a woman with a son. So I figured, if I'm gone..." Jesse shrugged. "Then there's nothing to stop you."

In other words, Mac realized, this running-away business was *his* fault. Shocked, he gaped at the boy. "You got it all wrong, Jesse. You're a great kid. None of this is about you or your mom. I know she understands that because we discussed it."

"Then how come she cried so much last night?"

"She cried?"

Jesse nodded. "She didn't think I heard her, but I did."

Now Mac felt worse than ever, so bad his heart seemed to have cracked. God, what a disaster. The least he could do was give Jesse the straight goods.

"I never meant to hurt her or you," he said. "The honest truth is, all my life I've taken care of other people. I didn't get to do the things I wanted, like travel and go to college. Instead, I raised Ian and Brian and worked. We had an agreement that when they finished school, it was my turn. They both graduated in December, and here we are."

"I didn't know you raised your brothers or that other stuff," Jesse said. "No one ever told me."

"I never thought about filling you in—my mistake. I guess because I didn't expect that things would… would go where they did. Your mom knew everything, though, from the first week we met."

At the time Mac had been so sure of what he wanted. He'd had it planned for years. But now… "Then we…liked each other and got involved and everything changed," he added.

With a knowing look, Jesse crossed his arms. "I thought so."

This next part was harder to admit. Mac swallowed audibly. Cleared his throat and continued. "I, uh…while I've been out looking for you, scared that you ran away and worried that you were in trouble, I realized something important." He looked straight at Jesse. "I care a heck of a lot about you. I care about your mom, too, more than I ever imagined."

In fact, he loved Emmy. Totally and completely. And wasn't that a stunner? Awash in feelings, Mac sat back and shook his head.

The boy scrutinized him as if he wasn't sure what to think of this. "That's good, right?"

"Yeah. It is." Scary, too.

Jesse nodded and uncrossed his arms. For the first time since climbing into the van, he relaxed in his seat.

Bowled over by his own amazing feelings, relieved that he and Jesse had come to an understanding of sorts, and knowing Emmy must be pacing her living room, waiting for her son, Mac clapped the boy's narrow shoulder. "I know your mom's anxious to see you. Let's head home."

During the mostly silent drive back, he did some thinking about what he really wanted, now that he'd admitted to himself that he loved Emmy. In light of his feelings for her and Jesse, his old dreams didn't seem as important as they once had. But he'd held on to them for such a long time. Could he really let them go?

As he turned onto Beach Cove Way, Jesse suddenly spoke. "You say you care about my mom and me. What are you planning to do about that?"

The question and his unflinching expression proved that this afternoon the boy had started down the path toward adulthood. Mac sensed that he'd grow into a fine man. And that was something he wanted to witness firsthand.

He saw his future clearly then, and suddenly everything fell into place. "If it's okay with you, I'd like to wait to answer that until we're inside so that both you and your mom hear what I have to say."

"Sure." Jesse made a face. "You know she's going to cry and get all mushy when she sees me."

"That's women for you."

His brothers' truck was parked out front. Fine with Mac. They should hear this, too. Nervous and excited, but no longer scared, he pulled into Emmy's driveway, braking behind her car.

Before the engine died, Jesse was out and hurrying toward the cottage.

Mac followed, standing just inside the door as Emmy and her son embraced, both tearful and talking at once. Emotional himself, Mac blinked hard.

His brothers wiped their eyes and nodded at the door, signaling they wanted to leave. Mac shook his head and gestured for them to wait.

"Promise me you'll never run away again," Emmy said, clasping Jesse's shoulders and peering into his face.

"I swear." Sniffling, Jesse pulled a wad of bills from his pocket. "This is yours. If you want to ground me, go ahead. I deserve it."

Emmy looked from her son to Mac. "Whatever you said to him, Mac, thank you. And thanks for bringing him home." She frowned at the boy. "Jesse Franklin Logan, you are grounded. No phone, no TV and no e-mail, no sleepovers with Peter for two weeks."

Her son nodded meekly.

Dabbing at her eyes, she glanced at Mac's brothers. "I'm also grateful to you two for looking for Jesse. And for being my friends."

Ian and Brian gave sober nods.

Jesse's eyebrows hitched up. Noticing, Mac's brothers eyed him curiously. *Showtime.*

Mac fiddled with the collar of his shirt. Shifted onto the balls of his feet. "I figured out something important tonight…" His voice actually cracked, and he started to tear up. Pausing, he pulled himself together. "Thing is, I care about you both." He glanced from Emmy to Jesse and back to Emmy. "A lot. I want you in my life for a long time."

Ian looked surprised, but Brian grinned.

"You know I feel the same way," Emmy said. "But you're leaving soon. If you're asking us to wait for you, the answer is yes."

Jesse nodded.

"I don't want that."

"Oh." Her face fell.

"Why should you wait for me to come back when I'd rather stay here with you?"

"But your plans—traveling and school…"

"About those. As we all know, you two—" Mac nodded at Ian and Brian "—hate the remodeling business. I don't want my company to die, but if I leave for three years, it will. I think I know a way to keep us all happy. I'll stay here and run the company and take online college classes." It wouldn't be the same as attending school full-time, but Mac no longer cared. "It'll take longer to get my degree, but that's okay. I'm in no hurry."

His announcement didn't seem to surprise anyone but Emmy. "But you've been dreaming of this for so long," she said with a quizzical look. "Are you sure?"

"Absolutely."

"What about traveling?"

"Plenty of time for that, too."

"You can't give up your trip," Emmy said. "Jess and I will wait for you."

Jesse nodded again.

"You could go for a few weeks," Brian suggested. "I

won't be starting school until fall, if I get in. I'm fine sticking around here."

"It'll take me a while to find the right computer-programming job," Ian said. "So go. We'll hold the fort till you get back."

Emmy's eyes widened. "Mac knows?"

Mac nodded. "You should've said something, Emmy."

"I wanted to, but I promised your brothers I wouldn't," she said.

"And I respect that you kept your word. But no more secrets between us, okay?" Mac smiled to show her he wasn't mad.

"I swear."

"Are you going to go away or not?" Ian asked.

Mac wasn't even tempted. Someday he'd travel. If all went well, with Emmy and Jesse. "For now, I'd rather stay here." He wanted to say more, but first he needed to touch Emmy. He closed the gap between them and clasped her hands. "I love you, Emmy." He let go of one hand to ruffle Jesse's hair. "You, too, kid."

"Oh, Mac!" Emmy's eyes shone. "I love you, too. I have for ages." She laughed. Cried. Then stretched up, pulled his head down and kissed him.

A long, satisfyingly loving kiss that made Mac hungry to be alone with her.

"Ahem," Jesse said, his mouth twitching.

Mac's brothers flashed their teeth in wolfish smiles.

Arm around his woman, Mac grinned broadly. He winked at Jesse, who gave a sober, manly thumbs-up. Then dropped the adult pose to hug Mac, hard. When they released each other, the boy was beaming.

"I assumed you'd all want to stay for dinner and

pulled an extra casserole from the freezer," Emmy said. "Shall I pop them both into the oven?"

"I'll do that for you," Ian said.

"And I'll set the table after I wash up." Brian rolled up his sleeves.

"I'll wash up, too, and then fix the ice water," Jesse chimed in. "You and Mac relax, Mom."

Keeping Emmy close to his side, Mac watched the people he cared for bustle about. All his hopes and dreams were right here in this little cottage with the woman he loved and her son. He'd never felt so happy or content.

Life was sweet.

* * * * *

*Celebrate 60 years of pure reading pleasure
with Harlequin!*

To commemorate the event, Harlequin Intrigue®
is thrilled to invite you to the wedding of The Colby
Agency's J. T. Baxley and his bride, Eve Mattson.

That is, of course, if J.T. can find the woman who
left him at the altar. Considering he's a private
investigator for one of the top agencies in the
country—the best of the best—that shouldn't be
a problem. The real setback is that his bride isn't
who she appears to be…and her mysterious past
has put them both in danger.

*Enjoy an exclusive glimpse of Debra Webb's
latest addition to*
THE COLBY AGENCY: ELITE
RECONNAISSANCE DIVISION

THE BRIDE'S SECRETS

Available August 2009 from Harlequin Intrigue®.

The dark figures on the dock were still firing. The bullets cutting through the surface of the water without the warning boom of shots told Eve they were using silencers.

That was to her benefit. Silencers decreased the accuracy of every shot and lessened the range.

She grabbed for the rocks. Scrambled through the darkness. Bumped her knee on a boulder. Cursed.

Burrowing into the waist-deep grass, she kept low and crawled forward. Faster. Pushed harder. Needed as much distance as possible.

Shots pinged on the rocks.

J.T. scrambled alongside her.

He was breathing hard.

They had to stay close to the ground until they reached the next row of warehouses. Even though she was relatively certain they were out of range at this point, she wasn't taking any risks. And she wasn't slowing down.

J.T. had to keep up.

The splat of a bullet hitting the ground next to Eve had her rolling left. Maybe they weren't completely out of range.

She bumped J.T. He grunted.

His injured arm. Dammit. She could apologize later.

Half a dozen more yards.

Almost in the clear.

As she reached the cover of the alley between the first two warehouses she tensed.

Silence.

No pings or splats.

She glanced back at the dock. Deserted.

Time to run.

Her car was parked another block down.

Pushing to her feet, she sprinted forward. The wet bag dragged at her shoulder. She ignored it.

By the time she reached the lot where her car was parked, she had dug the keys from her pocket and hit the fob. Six seconds later she was behind the wheel. She hit the ignition as J.T. collapsed into the passenger seat. Tires squealed as she spun out of the slot.

"What the hell did you do to me?"

From the corner of her eye she watched him shake his head in an attempt to clear it.

He would be pissed when she told him about the tranquilizer.

She'd needed him cooperative until she formulated a plan. A drug-induced state of unconsciousness had been the fastest and most efficient method to ensure his continued solidarity.

"I can't really talk right now." Eve weaved into the right lane as the street widened to four lanes. What she needed was traffic. It was Saturday night—shouldn't be that difficult to find as soon as they were out of the old warehouse district.

A glance in the rearview mirror warned that their unwanted company had caught up.

Sensing her tension, J.T. turned to peer over his left shoulder.

"I hope you have a plan B."

She shot him a look. "There's always plan G." Then she pulled the Glock out of her waistband.

Cutting the steering wheel left, she slid between two vehicles. Another veer to the right and she'd put several cars between hers and the enemy.

She was betting they wouldn't pull out the firepower in the open like this, but a girl could never be too sure when it came to an unknown enemy.

Deep blending was the way to go.

Two traffic lights ahead the marquis of a movie theater provided exactly the opportunity she was looking for.

The digital numbers on the dash indicated it was just past midnight. Perfect timing. The late movie would be purging its audience into the crowd of teenagers who liked hanging out in the parking lot.

She took a hard right onto the property that sported a twelve-screen theater, numerous fast-food hot spots and a chain superstore. Speeding across the lot, she selected a lane of parking slots. Pulling in as close to the theater entrance as possible, she shut off the engine and reached for her door.

"Let's go."

Thankfully he didn't argue.

Rounding the hood of her car, she shoved the Glock into her bag, then wrapped her arm around J.T.'s and merged into the crowd.

With her free hand she finger-combed her long hair. It was soaked, as were her clothes. The kids she bumped into noticed, gave her death-ray glares.

They just didn't know.

As she and J.T. moved in closer to the building, she grabbed a baseball cap from an innocent bystander. The crowd made it easy. The kid who owned the cap had made it even easier by stuffing the cap bill-first into his waistband at the small of his back.

Pushing through the loitering crowd, she made her way to the side of the building next to the main entrance. She pushed J.T. against the wall and dropped her bag to the ground. Peeled off her tee and let it fall.

His gaze instantly zeroed in on her breasts, where the cami she wore had glued to her skin like an extra layer. A zing of desire shot through her veins.

Not the time.

With a flick of her wrist she twisted her hair up and clamped the cap atop the blond mass.

"They're coming," J.T. muttered as he gazed at some point beyond her.

"Yeah, I know." She planted her palms against the wall on either side of him and leaned in. "Keep your eyes open. Let me know when they're inside."

Then she planted her lips on his.

* * * * *

Will J.T. and Eve be caught in the moment?
Or will Eve get the chance to reveal all of her secrets?
Find out in
THE BRIDE'S SECRETS
by Debra Webb.
Available August 2009 from Harlequin Intrigue®

We'll be spotlighting a different series every month throughout 2009 to celebrate our 60th anniversary.

LOOK FOR
HARLEQUIN INTRIGUE®
IN AUGUST!

To commemorate the event, Harlequin Intrigue® is thrilled to invite you to the wedding of the Colby Agency's J.T. Baxley and his bride, Eve Mattson.

Look for *Colby Agency: Elite Reconnaissance*

THE BRIDE'S SECRETS
BY DEBRA WEBB

Available August 2009

www.eHarlequin.com

REQUEST YOUR FREE BOOKS!

2 FREE NOVELS PLUS 2
FREE GIFTS!

Love, Home & Happiness!

YES! Please send me 2 FREE Harlequin® American Romance® novels and my 2 FREE gifts (gifts are worth about $10). After receiving them, if I don't wish to receive any more books, I can return the shipping statement marked "cancel." If I don't cancel, I will receive 4 brand-new novels every month and be billed just $4.24 per book in the U.S. or $4.99 per book in Canada.* That's a savings of close to 15% off the cover price! It's quite a bargain! Shipping and handling is just 50¢ per book. I understand that accepting the 2 free books and gifts places me under no obligation to buy anything. I can always return a shipment and cancel at any time. Even if I never buy another book from Harlequin, the two free books and gifts are mine to keep forever.

154 HDN EYSE   354 HDN EYSQ

Name _____ (PLEASE PRINT) _____

Address _____ Apt. # _____

City _____ State/Prov. _____ Zip/Postal Code _____

Signature (if under 18, a parent or guardian must sign)

Mail to the **Harlequin Reader Service:**
IN U.S.A.: P.O. Box 1867, Buffalo, NY 14240-1867
IN CANADA: P.O. Box 609, Fort Erie, Ontario L2A 5X3

Not valid to current subscribers of Harlequin® American Romance® books.

Want to try two free books from another line?
Call 1-800-873-8635 or visit www.morefreebooks.com.

* Terms and prices subject to change without notice. Prices do not include applicable taxes. N.Y. residents add applicable sales tax. Canadian residents will be charged applicable provincial taxes and GST. Offer not valid in Quebec. This offer is limited to one order per household. All orders subject to approval. Credit or debit balances in a customer's account(s) may be offset by any other outstanding balance owed by or to the customer. Please allow 4 to 6 weeks for delivery. Offer available while quantities last.

Your Privacy: Harlequin is committed to protecting your privacy. Our Privacy Policy is available online at www.eHarlequin.com or upon request from the Reader Service. From time to time we make our lists of customers available to reputable third parties who may have a product or service of interest to you. If you would prefer we not share your name and address, please check here. ☐

HAR09R

You're invited to join our Tell Harlequin Reader Panel!

By joining our new reader panel you will:

- Receive Harlequin® books—they are FREE and yours to keep with no obligation to purchase anything!
- Participate in fun online surveys
- Exchange opinions and ideas with women just like you
- Have a say in our new book ideas and help us publish the best in women's fiction

In addition, you will have a chance to win great prizes and receive special gifts!
See Web site for details. Some conditions apply.
Space is limited.

To join, visit us at
www.TellHarlequin.com.

HARLEQUIN® *Romance*®

Welcome to the intensely emotional world of

MARGARET WAY

with

Cattle Baron: Nanny Needed

It's a media scandal! Flame-haired beauty
Amber Wyatt has gate-crashed her ex-fiancé's
glamorous society wedding. Groomsman
Cal McFarlane knows she's trouble, but when
Amber loses her job, the rugged cattle rancher
comes to the rescue. He needs a nanny, and
if it makes his baby nephew happy, he's
willing to play with fire....

*Available in August
wherever books are sold.*

HRI7601

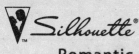
Silhouette®

Romantic
SUSPENSE

**Sparked by Danger,
Fueled by Passion.**

CAVANAUGH
JUSTICE

The Cavanaughs are back!

USA TODAY bestselling author

Marie Ferrarella

Cavanaugh Pride

In charge of searching for a serial killer on the loose,
Detective Frank McIntyre has his hands full. When
Detective Julianne White Bear arrives in town searching
for her missing cousin, Frank has to keep the escalating
danger under control while trying to deny the very
real attraction he has for Julianne. Can they keep their
growing feelings under wraps while also handling the
most dangerous case of their careers?

Available August wherever books are sold.

Visit Silhouette Books at www.eHarlequin.com

SRS27641

COMING NEXT MONTH
Available August 11, 2009

#1269 THE RODEO RIDER by Roxann Delaney
Men Made in America
A vacation was all attorney Jules Vandeveer needed to clear her head. But rest was the last thing on her mind when she met rodeo rider Tanner O'Brien. Jules was immediately drawn to the rugged cowboy, and her heart went out to him and his rebellious nephew. Helping them heal wasn't a problem…but for once, walking away would be.

#1270 MISTLETOE MOMMY by Tanya Michaels
4 Seasons in Mistletoe
Dr. Adam Varner planned this trip to Mistletoe to reconnect with his kids. When he rescued a stranded pet sitter with car trouble, he didn't expect Brenna Pierce to have such an amazing connection with his daughters and son. Brenna is the woman Adam didn't know he was looking for—can he make a temporary stay in Mistletoe into something more…permanent?

#1271 SAMANTHA'S COWBOY by Marin Thomas
Samantha Cartwright needs to access her trust fund to start up a ranch for abused horses. Wade Dawson needs to keep Samantha distracted until he can figure out where her missing money went! So Wade spends as much time at Sam's ranch as he can—and, with Sam, discovers his inner cowboy….

#1272 ONE OF A KIND DAD by Daly Thompson
Fatherhood
Daniel Foster has built his own family looking after foster kids. And when he meets Lilah Ross and starts to fall for her, he knows he wants Lilah and her young son to be a part of that family, too. But when Lilah's ex-husband threatens her son, Daniel is afraid he could lose them both.

www.eHarlequin.com

HARCNMBPA0709